Richard Pastor

A Texas Cowboy
in Tuscany

a novel

A Texas Cowboy in Tuscany is a work of fiction.
Names, Characters, places and incidents either are
products of the author's imagination or are used
fictitiously. Any resemblance to actual persons, living
or dead, events, or locales is entirely coincidental.

Book design and cover photography by Richard Pastor

Editor Jefferson Hancock

texastuscany@sbcglobal.net

Dedications

Without the following people this book would never have been written.

Sean and Anita for their unwavering friendship.

Kelly and Bob for their generosity and commitment to family.

Karen for her inspirational strength and Italian driving skills.

Craig for his encouragement and for grading my paper.

Vincente, my father for what I know of ranching and being a man.

Barbara Banke of Jackson Family Wines for her hospitality at the Arceno Wine Estate San Gusme Toscana, Italy.

Frances Mayes for her wonderful books on Tuscany, that brought me to the beautiful village of Cortona.

My thanks to you all.

A Texas Cowboy in Tuscany

A Novel

Written By Richard Pastor

Chapter 1
Calvert Texas, 1970

Standing on the front porch of his father's rundown ranch house, Randy took in his inheritance: a house; a ramshackle barn that leaned slightly towards the setting sun; and five hundred scrubby acres of South Texas land that hadn't been worked in over seven years.

His father's white and rusted Chevy pickup was parked next to the barn. It looked as it hadn't moved for decades. The right front tire was flat, weeds grew around the wheels, and it was covered with almost seven years worth of Texas dust. Randy had learned how to drive in that rusty old truck.

As he thought over his future, the memories of the past came flooding back.

Randy and his father Hank were repairing a break in the fence on the south end of the ranch when the elder cowboy tossed his son the keys.

"Could sure use a cold one." He said as he wiped the sweat from his face with a dirty blue bandana. "Run back to the house and fetch me a coupla beers will ya Randy?"

Randy looked at him with surprise.

"But Hank, I don't even know how to drive!"

"You'll figure it out. Besides, you can't hit nothin'," he said with that crooked smile of his.

There was no arguing with Hank. He was a man of few words and did not speak unless he meant what he said. So Randy eagerly slid behind the wheel, turned the key and stepped on the starter. The truck lurched forward, then died.

"You gotta push in on the clutch Randy. Remember? The one on the left," he said, without even turning around. Randy knew Hank was smiling, even though he could not see his father's face. He turned the key, using the clutch this time, and the motor roared to life.

"Now let it out slow and she'll take you back to the house on her own!"

Randy let out the clutch and the truck began its beer run. The kid could barely reach the pedals or see over the dashboard. He remembered sitting in Hank's lap and steering many times, but he'd never driven alone until now. The truck barreled down the dirt road towards the house with Randy, sporting a toothy grin, behind the wheel. The windows were down and cigarette butts bounced out of the full ash tray as clouds of brown Texas dust rolled behind the truck.

When Randy got back, carrying the two cold bottles of Lone Star his father had asked for, Hank threw his tools in the back and they sat on the soft, warm ground on the shady side of the truck out of the blistering Texas summer sun. Hank took one of the beers and popped the cap off on a corner of the truck bed.

"Here."

He handed Randy the cold bottle and the boy took it without a word. It was his first beer; he'd stolen a few sips before but never had one of his own. The boy opened the other bottle the same way as his father had the first. Chips of white paint and rust scraped off the bed as he did and a few snow-like flakes drifted to the ground. Hank looked at his son with a familiar smile and tapped his bottle with the boy's.

"See? Told ya it 'twern't hard." They drank deeply and Randy became a twelve-year-old man that day.

As long as Randy could remember it was just Hank and him. The boy never knew his mother because she left when he was a baby. Hank never talked about her and Randy never saw pictures of her, if there were any. As a kid he often wondered who and where she was. The kids at school would say this or that about their mothers and on parent-teacher nights he'd see the other parents sitting together while Hank grabbed a chair alone in the back of the room. At barbeques or Calvert Community events he'd see kids holding their moms' hands or sitting in their laps while the mothers held their children close or wiped ice cream or tears from their faces. "How come I don't have a mother?" he wondered. It was a persistent thought that crept in more often than he would've liked.

One evening after supper as father and son sat on the porch enjoying the cool dry autumn air, the boy asked Hank about his mother. His old man let out a heavy sigh, reached into the left pocket of his shirt and pulled out a familiar red and white pack of Lucky Strikes. Then he stuffed his hand into his jeans pocket and came up with his old scratched and dented Zippo lighter. As he lit the cigarette with that anticipated metallic snap of the Zippo, he leaned back lost in thought for a minute, a cloud of smoke circling the brim of his hat.

"Your Ma was a real looker Randy." He said "She had better things in mind than workin' this place with me."

"Why did you marry her then Hank?" the boy asked with honest curiosity.

Hank took in a drag of his cigarette, blew out the smoke and said, "I loved her Randy, simple as that," like it was the only answer there could be. He had a strange faraway look for a second or two, as though a memory had taken him out of this moment and laid him gently in another.

"She loved you too and don't you ever forget that."

He faced Randy then, looking square into the boy's eyes to make sure his words had sunk in.

"At least she left me a great goin' away present. The best present I ever got!"

He reached over and tousled his son's blonde hair roughly and smiled so big Randy thought his teeth would reach his ears. That was as close to 'I love you son' as he ever got from Hank, but after that night Randy never doubted it, not once. They never spoke of her again and Randy never felt the need to. Hank Bartlett was his dad and that was all Randy needed to know.

Now standing on that same porch years later, Randy reached into his pocket and pulled out Hank's battered Zippo. He brought it to his nose and took in the familiar smell of long gone lighter fluid and flint. It smelled of Hank. It smelled of home. It smelled of loss. He could feel his eyes filling.

No.

He won't allow the tears to come. Hank would not have approved.

Chapter 2

Henry James Bartlett was born and raised in Calvert, Texas. His mother and father came from Oklahoma to work in the cotton fields just before the Great Depression began and stayed on because The Dust Bowl had engulfed the plains and there was no work anywhere else. After years of toiling in the fields and sweaty warehouses his father scraped enough together to buy a five hundred acre plot of land just south of town and tried to make a go of growing cotton himself. Unfortunately for the Bartlett Family he was a much better laborer than he was a grower and the small plantation was a miserable failure.

Hank was still a teenager when his parents both died in the same year of influenza and left him the worthless cotton farm. Unable to work the farm alone Hank chose the only other option he had. World War Two was at its peak when seventeen year old Hank Bartlett lied about his age to join the Army.

For the next three years the handsome, lean young man from Texas fought a terrible war in the South Pacific that he did not understand, experiencing all the horrors that war could bring and more. By the time he was nineteen he was a hardened veteran. He had watched a good many of his buddies die gruesome deaths in bloody battles on tiny islands whose names he could barely pronounce. He'd also killed men by his own hand and was sickened each time it happened. Somehow, either through divine intervention or pure dumb luck, he survived when so many others did not. His body untouched but with unseen scars.

When the war finally ended Hank returned to Calvert a quiet and introverted man, still young in years but old in soul.

Thanks to his Depression-era upbringing, Hank had always been frugal, so he was able to save most of his Army pay during the war. With it he bought two hundred head of Angus beef cows and converted the old family cotton farm into a small working cattle ranch. The work was hard and the profits were meager but it soon became a labor of love for the quiet young man. The heavy labor suited him and the nightly exhaustion allowed him to sleep instead of lying awake in the dark alone with his memories of war.

The Army had taught him discipline and Hank was comforted by its security. He maintained those same rigid habits as a civilian because order was calming to him; without it, life was chaotic and unmanageable. He kept his home clean and organized, and he lived a quiet, regimented life for two years after his discharge.

Then fate stepped in and changed his safe life of work and routine.

Chapter 3

The fuel gauge was bouncing nervously on E when Hank pulled into the Texaco station on the Texas Six with his new white Chevy pick-up truck. Ahead of him in the gas island was a big green Buick convertible gleaming with polished paint and chrome. No one was in the car and Hank was unable to reach the pump. He waited a few minutes for the owner to return and move on but became impatient when after five minutes no one came back to the car. Hank got out of his truck and searched the station for the pimply faced kid that pumped the gas but he was nowhere to be seen.

He went into the cramped, messy office and passed through the connecting door to the garage. The lights were off and all was quiet except for the sound of his boots on the oily cement floor.

From inside the cool dark garage he heard muffled voices from around the back near the restrooms. "The kid must be taking a bathroom break," he thought, but when he rounded the corner of the building he found a large well dressed man arguing with a small blonde woman in a flowery dress. This was none of Hank's business so he turned back toward his truck. Not worth the trouble," he grumbled. "I've got enough gas to make it to the other station in town."

But the big man did something Hank couldn't ignore, slapping the blonde hard across the face with the back of his hand. Hitting a woman was high on the list of don'ts in Hank Bartlett's rule book.

He walked over to the big bully and shoved him hard.

"Hey, you fucking hayseed! What do think you're doing?" the man yelled. He was caught off balance and Hank's push almost knocked him over.

"Hands off the lady mister," Hank ordered, sizing up the big guy. The angry man was obviously no stranger to violence and needed to be watched carefully.

"Mind your own business, shit kicker!" the brut snarled, and he came toward Hank fast.

In the war Hank survived by using his head and his quick reflexes. When he felt himself in danger he acted quickly and decisively. He had not forgotten those skills in his short amount of time as a civilian.

The big man took a swing but was too slow and Hank easily stepped out of his way. The intended punch went wild and the man swung completely around exposing his ribcage which was exactly where Hank put his fist as hard as he could. He could feel the man's ribs crack on impact. Hank had learned that trick from a drunken Marine on leave in Australia. The Marine told him that was the quickest way to stop a big man because he can't keep fighting with broken ribs. Hank had watched the drunken soldier put his theory into practice in a bar fight once.

"Works every time," the seasoned Marine had told him with a satisfied grin.

The big man went down to his knees, hugging his torso wincing in pain with every breath he took.

"You broke my ribs you hick son of bitch!" the man yelled, but he regretted it because now he had to take in another deep and painful breath.

"Yes, I know. Works every time," Hank said, and he turned back to his truck. He got about half way to it when he heard the woman's voice.

"Wait!" she yelled and ran to catch up to Hank, her high heels clacking on the concrete.

"Can you give me a ride into the next town?"

"Yes ma'am. Hop in," Hank said keeping an eye on the man in case he tried to get up and follow them. He didn't.

She grabbed a small suitcase from the Buick, threw it in the back of the pickup and they left the large man on his knees at the station praying to the Texaco Star.

The ride into Calvert is only a few miles but Hank was not used to company while he drove and the unfamiliar situation felt uncomfortable and strange to him. He already looked forward to reaching town and letting his rider out.

He glanced over to the woman and she matched his look with her own. To her this eye contact was the queue for introductions.

"I'm June Sinclair," she said and held out her small hand adorned with heavily painted blood red fingernails.

"Hank," was all he said as he took it.

"Thank you for that back there, Hank. You are a real gentleman."

June smiled and her white teeth showed as slick white pearls against her shiny thick red lipstick that matched the shade of her nails. Hank did not respond to her thanks, nor did he return the friendly gesture of her smile.

June was not the type that enjoyed empty silences.

"We were on our way to Dallas after being in Galveston a few days. We met in New Orleans about three months ago. He was real nice to me then but he's got a short temper and I sure seem to piss him off a lot lately."

Her light perfume filled the cab of the pickup. It altered the very air he breathed. The familiar smell of the truck was replaced with the scent of roses and he was distracted by it.

"That's no excuse for hitting a woman." Hank said firmly.

"You get used to it." June said and she turned her face to the passenger window.

"You shouldn't have to." He looked at her now and as she faced him he could see her black mascara was running a little.

She took a small embroidered handkerchief from her pocket book and dabbed at her eyes while Hank looked straight ahead, pretending not to notice.

"Is there a bus stop in town?" she sniffled in mid sentence.

"Yes ma'am. Just across the road from the gas station in front of the diner. Bus comes by twice a day, mornin' and afternoon. One goes north and the other south." Hank told her.

They drove into Calvert and Hank spotted the familiar red and white 'Flying A' sign at the gas station in the middle of the small one-block downtown. Squat one and two story brick buildings weathered by years of wind and Texas dust lined both sides of the street. All the essentials were here: feed store, bank, grocery market, sheriff's office, post office, diner and a few small shops that catered to the simple needs or desires of the women in the area. A small dust devil spun drunkenly across the road as they reached the station.

Hank pulled up to the gas pump and recognized the short pudgy man in greasy coveralls and dirty baseball cap who came out to pump the gas.

"Hi'ya Hank!" The man said.

"Wayne." Hank touched the brim of his hat.

"Fill 'er up?" Wayne asked eager to please.

"Yeah. Much obliged, Wayne."

Hank got out and hurried around the front of the truck to the passenger door to open it for June. She watched him through the windshield as he crossed the front of the truck, giving him a slight look of surprise and an appreciative smile at this gentlemanly act. When he opened the door June swung her black silk stocking-covered legs out of the cab and stepped out onto the running board. Hank held his hand out and she took it for support as she stepped down like a lady, overplaying the role just a bit.

"Why thank you kind sir."

She smiled broadly now, and she sparkled in the noon day sun. Hank could not help but return it this time with his own rare smile.

He reached into the bed of his truck and pulled out her small brown roughed up suitcase. It was so light that he thought she must be wearing most of what she had with her.

Hank pointed out the blue Greyhound bus stop sign across the street in front of the diner. The running white dog promised speedy travel to one's destination of choice.

"Then I guess this is 'Good Bye' Hank," she said as she held out her tiny white hand.

Hank took her hand and held it for a second without really shaking it. She spun on her high heels and walked to the bus stop. Hank watched her swinging her battered little suitcase as she glided gracefully across the street. With her brightly colored dress lightly blowing about her small frame, she seemed out of place in this town of dusty jeans and muddy boots.

Hank paid Wayne for the gas and hopped back in his truck. Roses still hung in the air. June gave him a wave and a smile as he passed her on his way to the feed store. Without realizing it he found himself returning the wave.

The feed store was at the end of the short street and Hank went in with his supply list. Twenty minutes later he was loaded up and ready to head back to the ranch. A sudden hunger pang reminded him it was past lunch time. The diner was just down the block so he left his truck at the feed store and walked back toward it.

June was still standing under the bus stop sign and as he came up on her she gave him her warm smile once again. The thought struck him that she had little if any money and most likely had not eaten herself.

"Well, hello again," she said. "Isn't it awkward when you see someone again so soon after you have just said good bye?" It was more of an observation than a question.

"Hungry?" Hank asked.

"Are you buying?"

"Yes, I am."

"Then yes I'm very hungry."

She stepped up to the wooden sidewalk, hooked her arm around Hank's and they went into the diner together earning him looks from his neighbors having lunch in the small diner. They chose a table near the window and Hank held her chair as she sat.

They ordered two BLT's with french fries and Cokes. When the food arrived he waited for her to stop talking before he picked up his sandwich.

"I basically have two immediate problems, Hank." She nibbled the same fry for what seemed an eternity before reaching for another, lightly dipping it each time in ketchup before taking another tiny bite.

"First, when the bus comes I don't know which direction to go, north or south. Second, I have no money to buy a ticket so I guess the first problem doesn't really matter, does it?"

Her bright green eyes flickered between dipping her fries and Hank's face. Hank was watching them closely because he did not want to miss them when she looked up at him again. He suddenly realized he had not touched his food and began taking large bites from his sandwich while he listened to her speak. In just a few bites his was gone while hers looked as though small lipstick stained bites had been taken out of it by a child.

The roar of a diesel engine vibrated through the plate glass window of the diner accompanied by a thick cloud of dust that blew about the gigantic tires. The table shook and rattled the ice in their drinks. They both looked up as the bus had just pulled up, headed north for Dallas.

Before he had time to think about what he was saying Hank looked at her and said.

"I have an empty room at my ranch and need someone to cook and clean. Interested?"

"No funny business?" she asked very directly.

Hank blushed and promised her there would be none.

"Then it's a deal!"

She smiled again and they both watched as the bus drove away without June Sinclair on board.

The return drive was a little easier for Hank. He was getting used to June's company so having her in the truck did not seem quite so strange now. Even her perfume was becoming familiar and pleasant. Still his social skills were not quite up to par with hers so he relied on her to keep the conversation going. This was not a problem for her at all.

"I'm not a very good cook." She warned.

"Either am I."

"Do you have cows?"

"Yes ma'am. A few."

She wrinkled her nose a little and asked him.

"Do they smell bad?"

"Sometimes, yes ma'am." Hank said with the smallest crease of a smile.

"I've never really spent much time around animals. I have always lived in the city." She told him.

"They'll get used to you." She laughed at his joke and the sound of it made him wish he were a more clever man so he could hear it again.

They passed the Texaco station where they first met and both glanced over at it to be sure the big Buick was gone. He heard her let out a deep breath of relief but said nothing.

Soon they reached his ranch and Hank turned onto the dirt and gravel drive to the house.

He politely opened her door and helped her out. In her high heels, she wobbled on the soft dirt and loose gravel. It was apparent she was not wearing the proper shoes for the occasion.

Hank retrieved the key from the coffee can under the stairs and escorted his new employee into the house.

As they entered, June looked around the small living room and kitchen, commenting on how cute and tidy it was. Then he showed her to her room. His childhood bed with its bare mattress and white painted metal frame was still there in the corner, and his father's guitar lay propped in the opposite corner. Like the rest of house the small room was clean and neat as a pin.

"Where is the bathroom?" she asked Hank.

"The water and basin are at the kitchen sink and the outhouse is just out the back door."

"Outhouse?"

She looked at him, hoping for a joke, but none came.

"Yes ma'am." Hank said, not really expecting any objections, but it was obvious now one was coming.

She pulled back the lace curtains and peeked out the back door. She saw the little structure about twenty five yards away with a well worn path leading to it.

"That's going to be a problem for me, Hank. I need a real toilet and bath tub." She had not meant this to be an insult but Hank suddenly felt his home was inadequate. This was a new feeling for him, so he was embarrassed and even a little ashamed.

"Sorry ma'am, but this is all there is." He said, glancing down at the spotless kitchen linoleum-covered floor and shuffling his feet.

June realized she had unintentionally hurt him and said.

"Don't worry about it Hank. I'm just a silly city girl. I'll get used to it, I'm sure." But the damage was done and already Hank was thinking about what he could do to make her more comfortable. He brought her clean sheets, blankets, towels, and wash cloths.

By the time he had shown her the house and she had settled into her room the sun was beginning to cast a low shadow over the barn.

"I have to unload my truck and put the supplies in the barn so why don't you get supper ready?" he suggested.

After Hank left the house June surveyed the kitchen and its stock. She was definitely out of her element, but she searched for guidance among the few old cookbooks she found and set to work.

While Hank was working in the barn he could not get his mind off of June. He was neither stupid, nor blind and knew he was becoming infatuated with her. June was confident, social, open and friendly—all the things he was not. She was also sensitive and beautiful with a touch of helplessness thrown in. What man would not be infatuated? At the same time there was danger in her and he could sense it. She was the type of woman that would allow herself to be used and to use others if she needed to, not because she was cruel but because that was how she survived. He knew he was being manipulated unintentionally or even intentionally, and he cautioned himself to watch for that danger, but the warning lights were dimmed by his obvious crush on her.

Hank took the porch steps two at a time but as he opened the front door of the house smoke billowed into his face. He was frightened and called out, "June! June!"

He heard her crying and coughing but could not see her from all the smoke.

"June! Are you all right?" he yelled out again.

He traced the sound of her crying to the floor near the sink. He found her, lifted her to her feet, rushed her out to the front porch and sat her down. He could see she was not hurt and ran back into the house to deal with the kitchen fire. Luckily it was just a cast iron pan with burning bacon grease and he dealt with it quickly. He opened all the windows and doors to air out the house and went back out to the porch.

June was still sobbing and he sat next to her. He did not speak but simply waited for her to stop crying. When she finally did he said.

"I guess you're a worse cook than I am." He bumped her shoulder playfully with his.

She chuckled and wiped at her face, smearing her already ruined make up. Hank went into the house and came out with a damp towel. He wiped her tears and make up until most of it was gone. What he discovered underneath melted his heart. Here was the real June Sinclair, fresh faced and young. While her eyes were still red from crying and smoke, their green color was shining through like a pair of emeralds on the crown of a queen. Her lips were pink and soft and her lashes naturally long, the color of sun-dried hay. All of his warning lights were fading now.

"I'm sorry Hank," she sniffed.

"Don't worry about it. It's not the first time a pan has been burned on that stove." It was a lie and she knew it but she smiled at him anyway.

"There is something else I need to tell you." She looked up at him and brushed a curled lock of blonde hair from her face.

"I'm a girl in trouble Hank. Do you know what I mean?"

"Yes, I know what you mean." He paused and asked gently, "How far along are you?"

"About eight weeks." She said. "That's what we were fighting about at the gas station. I had just told him." She began to cry again. "I don't know what I'm going to do and I have nowhere to go."

"Yes you do," Hank said, and all of his warning lights went out completely.

Hank got June tucked into bed. She was drained physically and emotionally so was asleep in minutes. He on the other hand was not ready for sleep. He went through his evening ritual of washing and brushing but it did not provide the usual calming effect adhering to his routine usually did. His mind was not on his tasks. Instead he could think of nothing but the commitment he made to June tonight, a commitment that would most assuredly turn his life from simple and predictable to chaotic and complicated.

He needed a task to keep him grounded. He needed something that would maintain his focus and hold his mind steady. Suddenly he had it. He would build June a bathroom. But not just a bathroom, it would be a place she could go to have privacy and a little luxury. It would be a place where she could pamper herself, feel rejuvenated and beautiful. Hank stayed up half the night sketching and planning the new addition. He would begin tomorrow.

Before dawn broke Hank was tending to the cattle and his two horses. When his morning chores were done he drove into Bryan to the lumber yard. After getting what he needed to start his new bathroom addition he stopped at a department store and picked up a few things for his new guest.

He had traced her shoe on a piece of paper so had her shoe size but had to guess at the rest. He bought her jeans, boots and some women's work shirts. Nothing fancy but all the practical clothing she needed for life on a Texas cattle ranch. When he was satisfied with his choices he paid the clerk and drove back to the ranch. He was eager to begin his new project and was looking forward to seeing June.

Flipping a cigarette out of a rumpled pack of Lucky Strikes he drew it out of the pack with the corner of his mouth. With a snap of his Zippo and a spin of the flint wheel, a soft whoosh of the flame lit the hanging cigarette. The clap of the lighter as he closed it rang out as the cab of the truck filled with gray smoke. Even this small ritual gave him comfort. He would always congratulate himself if he performed it perfectly and this time he had.

As he pulled into the driveway he half expected to see the house burned to the ground from June's attempt at making lunch but that was not the case. The house was just as he had left it.

Hank came into the house with his packages and found June busy in the kitchen. She smiled brightly when she saw him and said, "Just in time!"

She had the table set and was bringing food to it.

"I hope you're hungry."

She was obviously proud of her achievement. Hank looked down at the fried bologna sandwiches, pickles and biscuits with white gravy. "An interesting choice," he thought.

"I brought you some things from Bryan. I hope they fit."

"Presents? For me?"

She beamed even brighter now and eagerly reached for the bags, pulling out the clothes Hank had bought her.

"How wonderful!" she squealed. "I'll be right back."

She rushed to her room and closed the door. A few minutes later she reappeared dressed in the new jeans and western shirt. Her pants were tucked inside her boots and her golden hair was pinned up. She put her hands on her hips and spun around theatrically.

"What do you think?" she asked Hank.

He was speechless and beads of sweat started forming on his brow. She looked beautiful in the form fitting jeans and tucked in shirt.

"You look very pretty, June," was all he could manage.

She made a small curtsy and said, "Thank you very much sir. Now please sit down and have your lunch before it gets cold."

The bologna was burnt around the edges, the gravy was lumpy and the biscuit was drier than a cow paddy in July but Hank did not care. It was the best meal he had ever eaten in his life.

That afternoon he began his bathroom project. He measured and staked out the perimeter. He marked the placement of the foundation blocks and where he would open the wall to the house. As Hank worked he became calm and focused. The precision needed for the job required his full attention and the rest of the world grew still and quiet. Each measurement and cut of the saw kept the world on track. Each nail driven held it together.

When he was in the war the screams and the gunfire could be silenced by finding a safe place he could be alone. He would take out his side arm, spread out a clean cloth and take the weapon apart piece by piece. Each piece was cleaned, inspected and oiled before being reassembled. A simple task performed over and over until he could do it blindfolded kept his mind occupied and kept him from giving in to the fear and the constant threat of death. It kept him sane in an insane war. Today, building June a bathroom gave him that same focus.

Over the next few days Hank worked extra long hours. Tending to the cattle and the new addition meant that he would work from before sunup and until after sundown. June insisted that she did not need him to work so hard for her comforts, but he needed to do this for her.

On the third day of his working marathon June put her foot down and demanded he take a break. She made him a special dinner of fried pork chops, mashed potatoes with gravy and green beans. Clearly she was perfecting her kitchen skills and Hank applauded her until she was forced to take a bow in the small kitchen. She shined with pride.

That night he once again could not find sleep. This time it was not his memories that kept him awake but thoughts of the woman in the next room. He imagined being with her in every way a man could be with a woman. He was becoming more than infatuated with every passing day. These were his final thoughts before drifting off to sleep with dreams waiting in the wings to torture him once again.

June was asleep in her too small bed when she heard the scream. It jerked her awake and she was instantly alert, a practice that had saved her life on more than one occasion. The sound was coming from the other room. She rose cautiously and reached for the bedroom door. As she opened the door another heart wrenching scream erupted from Hank's room.

"Get down! Take cover!" he yelled out.

"Medic! Medic!" he cried out in desperation.

She cracked open the door to his room and in the dim light she could see him laying on his back, his chest rising and falling, the air rushing in and out of his lungs. She cautiously approached his bed and could see he was drenched in sweat, his dripping hair matted to his head.

"He's hit! Sarge! He's hit!" Hank shouted.

June sat on the edge of his bed not knowing what she should do. He was having a torturous nightmare and she feared for him. She reached out her small hand and placed it on his sweat soaked chest.

Hank suddenly sat straight up eyes wide and breathing heavily. He brought his hands to his face and openly wept.

"Hank?" she said softly." It's alright. It was just an awful dream." She wrapped her arms around him and held him until he was calm again. He was safe in her arms and it soothed him. June let him go and went to the kitchen. She came back with a cold compress and laid it upon his forehead.

"I'm sorry." he said, still breathing heavily.

"Don't be."

"Thank you, June."

He was exhausted and closed his eyes. She stayed with him until he fell back to sleep.

When morning came Hank was still groggy. He vaguely remembered June caring for him when he was in the grip of one of his horrific dreams. He was slow at his morning chores and when they were almost finished he decided to rest a while and laid down on the seat of his truck with his boots hanging out the driver's side window and his hat pushed over his eyes.

Hank's thoughts shifted once again to June. Pregnant and alone she had few options. She would soon start to show and life would begin to focus on a new baby coming into the world. Just a few days ago his simple existence had none of these complications but he couldn't imagine going back to it now that it had been disrupted by this lovely stranger. He drifted off to a dreamless sleep.

He felt a tapping on the sole of his boot. When he pulled his hat up June's smiling face was peeking into the truck.

"Are you going to sleep the day away, Cowboy?" she teased.

"What time is it?" Hank asked, sitting up.

"It's almost noon. You had a rough night."

"I want to thank you for that." His embarrassment was showing on his face.

"I didn't do anything." June said.

"Yes, you did."

June smiled broadly. Hank could see her eyes were red and a little puffy like she had been crying.

He got out of his truck, came around to her side and stood close.

"Were you in the war, Hank?"

"Yes." He said as he leaned on the sun heated fender of the Chevy and lit a cigarette.

"Was it terrible?" June asked him and sat on the fender next to him.

"Yes it was."

She reached out her hand and laid it on his shoulder.

"I'm sorry," she said.

"Sometimes if you talk about the worst thing that has happened in your life the others seem smaller. What was the worst thing you remember, Hank?"

He was still for a moment, took a drag from his cigarette, and answered her question.

"We had just taken a small island that had been held by the Japanese for the last few years. At one time there were over 5,000 men there. When the war started turning our way Japan stopped sending supplies to the island. The enemy had hardly any food or ammunition but still they wouldn't surrender. We killed over three thousand of 'em.

"I left my foxhole and stepped into the trees to take a leak when six of the bastards attacked. Their teeth were bared and they were screamin' and chargin' at me with fixed bayonets. They'd been starvin' and their uniforms were in shreds, hangin' loose on their skinny bodies. I'd left my rifle behind and only had my side arm, so I fired at 'em twice. The first shot passed through the neck of the lead man and hit the man behind him in the chest. Blood sprayed from the wounded guy's neck but he still he ran a couple more yards before he fell. The man behind him went down clutching his chest. The second shot hit a third guy in the head and he went straight to his knees for a second then fell forward onto his face with his arms at his side like a rag doll. The other three got taken out by gunfire from another foxhole.

"When it was all quiet I walked over to the guy with the chest wound and stood over him. He was lying on his back coughing blood and a large, red pool was forming underneath him from where the bullet exited his body. His hands were shakin' as he reached into his shirt pocket and pulled out a picture of a young woman and child. He held it close to his face with his bloody hands. Between coughs and spasms he would say over and over, '*Watashi no ai sayōnara. Watashi no ai sayōnara.*'

"A minute or so later he stopped saying it and just stared at the picture. It was then I realized his eyes were staring but they were not seeing. He was dead. I picked up his weapon and pulled the clip. Empty. No bullets. He came at me with only his courage.

"I reached down and took the photo from his hands and wiped off the blood. She was so young and beautiful. The child was a handsome boy smiling for his father. I had just killed her husband and the boy's father. I slipped the picture back into his pocket, sat down next to the dead man and cried. I cried for him, for his family, for all the friends I had lost and for myself. Later, I asked a Japanese prisoner that spoke some English what '*Watashi no ai sayōnara*' meant. He told me it meant 'Goodbye my love.'"

Hank looked into June's eyes and saw genuine compassion.

"Sometimes when I remember I can push it away by focusing on something else, but the dreams feel like I'm still there, living it all over again."

June replaced her hand on his shoulder with her head and said no more. It was the perfect thing to do. They were quiet for a minute as he wiped his eyes.

Hank went back to the barn to finish his chores. When they were done he closed the barn doors and joined June sitting on one of the white washed wicker chairs on the porch.

"I have some errands to run in Bryan. Would you like to get dressed up and go? I'll buy you a nice dinner."

"You just don't want to eat my cooking," she said and pretended to be hurt.

"No! That's not it at all. I like your cooking!" He was terrified he had hurt her feelings.

"Liar," June said, and she giggled like a little girl.

Hank was relieved she was only joking.

"Why don't you put on one of your nice dresses and we can go right away."

"Alright, I will be ready in a jiff."

She ran into the house.

Hank followed and went to his room to change. He put on his best jeans, black dress boots and his white H BAR C ranch shirt with the pearly snap buttons. He went to his drawer and took out the only pieces of jewelry he owned, his turquoise bolo tie and his parents' gold wedding bands. He put on the tie and slipped the rings in his pocket. He put on his hat and looked at himself in the dresser mirror. The hat was sweat stained and dirty.

"This just won't do," he said to himself and he left it behind.

Hank went out to the truck and lit up a cigarette while he waited for June. Finally she emerged from the house wearing a billowy light yellow dress holding her high heeled shoes in one hand, pocket book in the other. She was still wearing the boots Hank had given her.

"Do you like this dress?" she said, fishing for a compliment.

"You look beautiful but what about the boots?" Hank asked.

She twirled her dress and stomped the boots on the porch. She held up her high heeled shoes laughed and said.

"I can't walk in the gravel with these on silly." She clomped down the porch steps, boot heels pounding on the worn wood and crunching over the coarse gravel to the truck. Hank opened the door and she slid in, rear first. She sat in the truck and held out her foot smiling at him expectantly without saying anything. Hank understood she wanted him to pull off her boots and he obliged her but rolled his eyes in mild protest. After she changed her shoes Hank closed the door and ran around to the driver's side. They headed down the driveway on their way for an afternoon in town.

June was chatty and in good spirits. She was excited about a day off the ranch and going to a large town where she could feel more like herself. There were some serious things Hank wanted to discuss with her but he did not want to spoil her good mood. The drive to Bryan was only about thirty minutes and what he had to tell her could wait until then.

They turned off the highway and drove into downtown Bryan. Hank stopped in front of Baskin's Western Wear and got out.

"I need to buy something. Want to come?"

"Shopping? Of course!" she said and did not wait for him to open the door for her. She was almost giddy at the thought of going shopping.

They went into the store together and Hank wandered over to the hats. She watched him as he tried on a few.

"I need two," he said to her. "I need one for wearing to town and one for dress up occasions."

He would put one on and June would shake her head or wrinkle her nose in disapproval. He tried on a black felt Stetson and she nodded at his choice. Then he tried on a straw rancher's hat and she approved so he bought them both. Hank thanked her for helping him choose and for her good taste. In return she kissed his cheek and told him how handsome he looked in his new hats. They returned to the truck and Hank drove a few more blocks then stopped in front of the Brazos County

Courthouse. He turned off the engine and she eyed him with curiosity.

"June I have something to ask you but I want you to listen to me first," he said with a serious tone and she looked at him with a worried frown, her happy mood faded along with her smile.

"Pretty soon we'll need to get ready for the baby. You'll need a doctor to be sure everything is alright with the both of you. As a single woman having an illegitimate child it won't be easy for you. People will treat you with disrespect and I can't stand for that."

She was looking at him and her eyes were beginning to fill as he reminded her of the difficult situation she was in. Hank reached into his pocket and took out the two gold bands. He reached out to her, took one of her dainty hands in his and opened her fingers. He laid the small ring in her palm.

"Now, I know you don't love me June but my feelings for you get stronger every day. I promise to protect you and your child and treat it as though it were my own. You would both have my name and no one need ever know. I don't have much but I can offer you and your child this."

The tears that were threatening to fall now trickled down her cheeks.

"Oh, Hank. You would do that for us?"

"I would be honored to June."

She leaned over and wrapped him in her arms, holding onto him, not speaking, with her head on his shoulder. He could hear her sniffing away her tears and could feel their warm dampness through his shirt.

"No one has ever shown me the kindness that you have, Hank," she said, still resting her head on him.

"This is the greatest gift anyone has ever offered me. Except for my black high heels of course." They both laughed and the tension was broken.

"I would be proud to share your name, Hank."

Hank was elated.

"Then let's go!"

"You mean now?"

"Well, we're here aren't we?" he said as he put on his new black Stetson.

"Ok! Why not?" she said.

Hank jumped out of the truck and let her out. He grabbed her hand and pulled her up the brick steps to the courthouse door.

After filling out the proper paperwork, Hank and June were standing in front of the Justice Of The Peace and he was performing one of his more enjoyable responsibilities.

"Do you Henry James Bartlett take June Rose Sinclair as your lawfully wedded wife?"

"I do."

"And do you June Rose Sinclair take Henry James Bartlett as your lawfully wedded husband?"

"I do."

"Then by the power vested in me by Brazos County and the State of Texas, I now pronounce you man and wife. You may kiss the bride."

Smiling broadly, the Justice of the Peace nodded at the groom expectantly.

Hank was suddenly struck by the realization that this would be their first kiss and was he was more nervous about that than he was about getting married! June saw his fear and shyness, so she brought her arms around his neck and pulled him gently to her lips. Time stood still for Hank as he was in the embrace of his bride. What was a harmless infatuation just days ago had blossomed into a love he had never known. In a short time this woman was suddenly the center of his universe.

Hank and June celebrated their wedding with a wonderful dinner at the best restaurant in Bryan. He stared at her from across the table as she excitedly talked of the places she'd been and the cities she'd seen. This was her world, the world of parties, music and nightlife. She had no real responsibilities except to enjoy life. This was how she lived and she loved it.

It was late by the time they left town and drove back to the ranch. June was asleep on his shoulder and the weight of her head comforted him. She woke as they turned onto the gravel drive.

"Wait here," he whispered to her.

Hank unlocked the door to the house, left it open and returned to the truck. He opened the door for her held and out his hand. As she took it and stood on the running board he brought his arm around her small waist, under her legs and lifted her. How light she was! He carried her up the steps and into the house easily. When he let her down she held on for a moment and looked into his eyes.

"You make me feel special Hank. No man has ever made me feel that way before."

"You are special, June. I hope one day you'll believe that." She let him go, went to her room and closed the door. Hank stood alone in the living room for a moment then went to his room. His bedtime ritual seemed pointless now. He did not feel the need to perform the methodic habit because his mind was already calm, filled with thoughts of June and not of the ghosts of war. He undressed, got into bed and lay awake in the dim light as the silver moon shown through the window.

The sound of the knob turning drew his eyes to the door. June stood in the doorway wearing a small lacy nightgown. Her blonde hair was reflecting the moonlight and it was as though the glow were coming from her instead of the moon. He could see her naked body through the nearly transparent lace. She padded barefoot over to the bed, pulled back the covers and slid in along side of him. As she pushed her body up to his, he could feel her cool skin.

"We can't sleep alone on our wedding night, Hank," she said softly.

"I didn't want to pressure you June."

"I am here because I want to be." She breathed into his ear. Hank turned and held her in his arms. He kissed her like he had never kissed a woman before because he had never loved before. He slid his hand under her gown and felt her smooth skin as he gently stroked her back. She sat up, pulled her nightgown over her head and tossed it away. Her small round breasts begged to be touched, and as he did so his desire for her rose tenfold.

She lay back down on the bed and he drew himself to her petite firm body. With her arms around him she raised her leg and wrapped it around his back. She was opening herself to him and it was an invitation he accepted eagerly. Hank was slow and gentle even though his hunger for her was rising. She felt so tiny in his arms he was afraid he might hurt her, but when she felt him close she drew herself onto him with a soft breathy moan. As he moved against her he felt her other leg hugging his back as she returned his movements.

Hank wanted to be with her like this forever but his urge for release was rising and he knew it was a tide that could not be held back for long. She could see his struggle for control and she placed her hands on his face drawing back his sweat dampened hair. She smiled and even moved faster against him.

"Let it come, Hank," she whispered.

That was all he needed to break his concentration and the tide rushed in. The physical desire combined with the love he felt for her gave him the most powerful orgasm of his life. His body was racked by the convulsion of the intense release and he cried out. She held him tightly until she felt the throbs inside of her cease.

Hank looked into her eyes and said.

"I love you June."

"I know you do, Hank, and I thank you for that with all my heart," she said.

Hank woke early, as usual, but this morning he was not alone. June was lying next to him, still asleep. He saw her angelic face in the predawn light and his heart swelled with love as he watched her sleep. His did his best to dress and slip out without disturbing her.

His morning chores could not wait and the livestock needed tending. As he closed the door with a light click of the latch, June's eyes were open.

Hank's body went through the motions of getting his work done but his mind was full of images and emotions of his new wife. He knew she didn't love him, but that was alright for now. Call it hope or dream but he wanted that love for him to grow naturally. For now all he could do was care for her and protect her.

His chores completed, he returned to the bathroom addition. The work was going well. The outside walls were finished and it was time to open the interior wall and begin the plumbing and electrical work. It was now more important to him than ever that June have these simple comforts to sustain her. She came to him while he worked, pleasant but not cheerful.

"All of this is for me?" she asked.

Hank looked up from his work, smiled and said, "Everyone deserves a quiet place to go to, June. This'll be yours."

She laid her hand on his shoulder as he was crouched on the floor. Her touch electrified him but he tried not to show it.

"I don't deserve this Hank. You do too much," she said with a solemn tone.

He stood and faced her.

"You deserve all I can give and more, June."

Hank kissed her forehead and went back to his work.

As the weeks passed they fell into a routine of work and small talk. Hank's nightly exhaustion often left June alone with her thoughts. Her pregnancy was progressing and she was beginning to show it. An obstetrician in Bryan was chosen and regular check-ups were made.

Hank continued to work on the bathroom but no longer allowed her to see the progress. He wanted it to be a surprise, so once the new door was installed he kept it locked even though she protested. He often teased her with the key until she pouted, but he did not give in.

One afternoon June was at the sink preparing lunch when Hank reached around her from behind. He kissed her neck and rubbed his hands on her growing belly as he so often did these days.

"It's finished." He whispered in her ear.

She turned quickly to face him. A slow smile appeared on her face as the thought of a hot bubble bath danced in her head. She was as excited as a child on Christmas morning anticipating the presents to come. He took her hand and guided her to the new bathroom door. He placed the key into her hand, smiled and stood away. She anxiously slipped the key into the lock, turned it and pushed open the door.

The large window poured light onto the gleaming surfaces. A large soaking tub promising soothing baths to come dominated one side of the room. Crisp lacy pale blue curtains blew in a warm breeze and their shadows danced across the white painted cabinetry and pedestal sink with its shining chrome faucet. The walls were tiled midway up and were glossy white with accent tiles of blue randomly set. The toilet was surrounded by a plush blue terrycloth rug so her bare feet would not be chilled by the smooth marble floor. A small powder room with a vanity and mirror was set in an alcove with a stool inviting her to sit and apply her rich creams and make up. Colorful bottles of bath salts, shampoos and soaps were lined up and waiting to be used. Along the far side of the wall was a large closet that begged her to go shopping and fill it with beautiful clothes. The top shelf was stacked with fresh white fluffy towels and wash cloths.

June walked in and stood in the center of the sparkling room. She looked at Hank who smiled delightedly as he watched her reaction to his gift. It was not what he expected. She covered her face and began sobbing uncontrollably. He rushed to her and held her close as she cried into his chest. Hank was totally confused and waited for her to compose herself. June looked up and met his concerned and questioning eyes.

"I don't deserve this gift, Hank, or the love you've given me," she said through her tears.

"I am the one who does not deserve you, June. This is nothing compared to what you have given me," he said as he held her at arms' length, looking deeply into her eyes. Then he sniffed the air and said, "I think you need a bath."

She laughed through her tears and pushed him to the door.

Hank was right. The new bath became her sanctuary. It refreshed her and lifted her spirits. She would spend hours soaking and pampering herself, emerging happy and restored. It pleased him to see her enjoy herself and freed him from the guilt of forcing her to use the outhouse. He himself did not use the new facility. His habits continued as always which was just fine with him.

Hank drove her to her doctor appointments and sat nervously in the waiting room until she was finished. At each visit all went well and she was told simply to continue to eat healthy food and get plenty of rest; the baby would come soon enough. It was already making its presence known with strong kicks and rolling movements. June soon grew too big for her jeans, so Hank took her to the department store to buy some maternity clothes. She cried when she first wore them, complaining that they made her look fat, but she soon got used to them.

Hank was in the barn when June came in, sat on a hay bale, and watched him work. The warm sun coming in from the big doors brightened the normally darkened windowless space and she saw Hank as he went about his chores. He was shirtless and sweating with dust and hay stuck to his slick damp skin. How healthy and strong he looked. This work meant something to him and that only added to his strength. Her child could only benefit from such a simple life. Her old life would not be right for the baby. With the way she moved from city to city and the company she kept, her son or daughter would not have a home and people to depend on. No, she decided. Her child would not live as she was forced to live. It would be safe and would be loved as she never was.

June was in the kitchen preparing lunch when a sudden pain doubled her over. Warm clear liquid ran down her legs and pooled on the floor. Her water had broken and now the baby would be coming soon. Suddenly she was terrified.

"Hank!" she called out. He must have been in the barn or somewhere else on the ranch and couldn't hear her. She could not bear the thought of going into labor alone, so she went to the front door and stood out on the porch. His truck was here that meant he was nearby, thank God for that.

"Hank!" she hollered again. This time he emerged from the cool darkness of the barn. He was already running toward her when another strong contraction came on.

"Ohhh!" she moaned loudly.

Hank reached her with concern on his face but he was not panicked. In fact he was just the opposite.

"How many so far?" he asked calmly.

"Only two," she groaned. "But they were big ones and my water broke."

"How far apart?"

"Only a few minutes." She looked at him now frightened.

"We had better get to the hospital," he said.

Hank grabbed the overnight bag they had already prepared and helped June into the truck as another hard contraction struck.

"Ohhh!" she moaned again. "It hurts Hank!"

"It will be okay, June; it's supposed to hurt."

She had four more powerful contractions by the time they got to the hospital in Bryan. The baby was coming fast!

The nurse at the desk called June's doctor, got her settled into her room then told Hank to go to the waiting area.

"Nooo!" she screamed. "Don't leave me, Hank!"

Hank begged the nurse to let him stay until she finally agreed. "Just until the doctor comes," she said, wagging a finger at him.

Hank sat next to June, holding her hand, and she squeezed his as tightly as she could, breathing heavily. Sweat streamed from her forehead, stinging her eyes. He pried her fingers loose from his and went to the bathroom. When he came out he had a washcloth soaked in cool water. He placed it on her head.

"I'm really scared, Hank," she said. Her green eyes pleaded with him to make the pain go away. Just then she could feel a freight train of a contraction coming down the track.

"Here comes another one!" she yelled. It was the biggest one yet and she cried out.

Hank sat with her on the bed and held her hand.

"It's alright, June. It will be over soon," he reassured her. Just then the doctor arrived.

"Alright Mr. Bartlett you had better wait outside." It was obvious he had dealt with new fathers many times before and did not like them in the way.

"Please doctor. This is her first baby, and she really is scared. Can't I stay with her?"

"You're not going to faint or get in the way, are you?" The gray haired doctor looked at him over his bifocals.

"No sir."

"Alright you can stay, but don't make any trouble."

Hank thanked him.

The doctor examined June and said, "You are just about ready to start pushing young lady, but not until I say. Understand?"

She nodded just as the Midnight Special of contractions roared into the station and she yelled.

"OOH!"

"Alright, that did it. I want you to push hard on the next one," the doctor said loudly to get her attention. Hank dabbed sweat from her forehead and face.

"You are so brave, June," he said. "You're doing great, Honey." His soothing voice calmed her fear.

"Here it comes!" she yelled out.

"Push hard June!" the doctor yelled back.

She leaned forward and pushed as hard as she could and she screamed through her gritted teeth. She looked at Hank with frightened eyes.

"I can't do it, Hank! I just can't!" she cried.

"Yes you can June. You're the strongest person I've ever known. I know you can do it!"

"The baby's head is crowning now, so push again, June! Hard!" the doctor said firmly.

She pushed until she thought she would turn herself inside out.

Then there was a cry. It was not a cry of pain or sorrow but one of arrival.

"It's a boy," the doctor announced.

The attending nurse wrapped the newborn and presented him to his mother.

June was in awe of her new son. Suddenly nothing else mattered. There was no pain or fatigue, only his tiny features, his nose, his ears and his perfect little fingers. She was laughing and crying at the same time.

Hank's face showed equal parts love and pride.

"He's beautiful June," he said as he kissed her forehead. She looked up at him and said, "Thank you Hank. Thank you so much for everything." It almost sounded like a goodbye.

The baby was in the nursery and June was resting in her room when Hank entered with his flowers. Her eyes were closed and he did not want to wake her so he started to leave when she said, "I'm awake, Hank. Come and sit with me."

The exhaustion was gone from her face and she looked like her old self.

"You were amazing June. I'm so proud of you," Hank said.

"I could not have done it without you Hank," she said, reaching out her hand to him. He took it.

"What's his name?" Hank asked her.

"I haven't decided. Any ideas?"

"How about your father's name?" he suggested.

"No. He was a real bastard. That's why my brother and I ended up in a foster home. We were very close when we were young but he died." She had never mentioned this before but Hank could tell it was something she did not like to talk about.

"What was his name?"

"Randy," she said, then smiled at him. "That's perfect! Randall Henry Bartlett."

The sound of his name given to the baby warmed Hank's heart and lumped his throat.

"I'm honored June." He kissed her with quivering lips.

June and the baby spent two days in the hospital and then Hank took them home. When they entered the house he brought her to the smaller bedroom. She opened the door and could not believe her eyes. In just two days Hank had transformed the little room into a beautiful nursery complete with bassinette, crib and rocking chair. The walls were painted a pale blue and the changing table was well stocked with diapers, pins and powder.

"It's lovely Hank," she said and kissed his cheek.

"But how ever did you do this so fast?"

"Sleep is over rated," he said and they both laughed.

The passing months were filled with midnight feedings and diaper changes. June proved to be an attentive mother and spent every waking moment with the new baby. She reacted to every sound he made, rocked him to sleep and stared at his perfect face until she knew every bump and crease of his skin.

One night Hank woke to the sound of crying. He rose from his bed and slowly opened the bedroom door. June was in the nursery rocking the baby. Her face was buried in the sleeping infant's swaddled belly, muffling her sobs. Hank elected not to interrupt this private moment, but June's deep sadness was becoming an increasing worry. He had heard this was normal in new mothers but it seemed to him to be more than a case of 'Baby Blues.' He decided he would talk to her doctor about it.

It was a busy time for Hank. Much of his small herd had reached full maturity and it was time to bring the cattle to market. He had contracted a truck and trailer crew to load and deliver them to the auction yard today. He had three hundred and fifty head and all but fifty were being sold.

He was up long before June and Randy and would not be back until late. He looked at her while she slept and she seemed so peaceful now, but her constant sadness frightened him. He would make a point to call her doctor tomorrow.

As he closed the door June opened her eyes. She was getting very good at feigning sleep these days. She got up as soon as she heard Hank leave and checked on the baby.

On horseback Hank drove the herd into the corral, up the chute and into the trailers. It took six trailers to haul the cattle to the Brazos Valley Stockyard in Bryan. The herd was healthy and well fed so he expected to get an excellent price at the auction.

By the time he got back to the ranch it was late afternoon. Hank was in a good mood. He had done well at the auction and was looking forward to telling his wife all about it. As he pulled into the driveway he saw a middle-aged, heavy set Mexican woman sitting on the front porch in one of the old white wicker chairs. She smiled as he got out of the truck and walked over to her.

"Buenas tardes Señor Bartlett. I am Carmen Hernandez," she said, rising from her chair as he approached her.

"Buenas tardes, señora. Porque estas aqui? Why are you here?" Hank asked her.

"Señora Bartlett asked me to stay with the baby until you returned. Here is my phone number if you need me to come back. I do not live far." She picked up her large colorful handbag and stepped down from the porch. She was smiling at him as she started walking down the drive to the road.

Hank stood there for a moment frowning at the slip of paper the woman gave him wondering where June was. He went into the house and looked in on Randy, who was asleep in his crib. When he came back into the kitchen he noticed an envelope on the kitchen table propped up between the salt and pepper shakers with "HANK" written largely on the outside. He tore it open and began reading.

Hank,

Please don't hate me. I could not bear it if I knew that you did. I don't know what I would have done had you not came along to rescue me. You saved my life and it is a debt I will never be able to repay. You have given me so much in the past year even though I did not deserve any of it. All you asked for in return was my love and I could not even give you that. I tried to fit into your life but I just couldn't do it. Everything just seemed so wrong. It felt as though I was right handed and it was tied behind my back and I was forced to use only my left.

Randy is the only good thing I have ever done and I love him too much to take him with me. His home is here with you. I free you from your promise to always protect me but I am begging you not to take back your promise to protect him and raise him as your son. If you do you will never be alone again. I know you will be a wonderful and loving father. Teach him how to be as good a man as you are. I could not ask for anything more because you are the finest man I have ever known. I know I have hurt you and I will never forgive myself for that.

I am so sorry I came into your life Hank but I thank God you came into mine.

Love always,
June

Hank just stood in the kitchen reading the letter again and again until Randy's crying snapped him from his trance. He went into the nursery and picked him up. Hank sat in the rocker and he and his son cried together. They were both missing the same person they loved most in the world.

Chapter 4

When you grow up in Calvert Texas and get to high school there are only a few interests for young men in the area: girls, cattle, horses, football and the price of cotton, not necessarily in that order. Since Randy was a big kid football was an easy choice. The coaches encouraged him to play offensive guard. It was a position that suited him. He was not a guy who liked the limelight so had no interest in playing quarterback or halfback. He liked the fact that he had a job to do and it was clear. If he did his job right the play would execute as planned. Let someone else carry the ball and have the glory. It made him feel like he was in control without standing out. He wasn't great but did his job and was good enough and so earned the respect of his teammates.

The quarterback of the Calvert Trojans that year was Antonio (Tony) Swanson, a handsome dark haired kid who moved there from Houston in his sophomore year. His family was well off and they had a big spread west of town. The girls took to him right away, the guys not so much. He was smaller framed than Randy was but muscular and smart. He had a strong arm and could throw a forty-yard pass with pinpoint accuracy. He also had a wicked sense of humor that made him a few friends but even more enemies. Most would say he was just a smartass.

On a hot August morning the team was at practice getting ready for the coming season. The coach had ordered two-a-days and this was only the morning session.

"Hey! Bartlett! Think fast!"

About the same time Randy heard his name he felt a jolt hit the back his helmet with such force he staggered forward and hit the ground hard. He looked up and saw Tony laughing his ass off. Randy stood up, scooped up the football that had hit him and slowly walked over. But he wasn't laughing. As he got closer, Tony could see how pissed off his offensive guard was and his smile faded.

"Take it easy, Bartlett. It was just a joke."

"Funny." Randy said sarcastically. "I wonder how far this ball will fit up your ass, Swanson. What do you think?" he said through his teeth while tossing the ball up and down in one hand. Randy could see Tony's eyes darting back and forth looking for some support. He found none. Most of the team would get a laugh out of watching Randy kick the shit out of his quarterback.

He took a few steps back as Randy came closer.

"Look, Bartlett," he said. "You don't really want to hurt the starting quarterback do you? Think of the team, the school and the town. How do you expect us to beat Bryan High with a football stuck in my ass?" His smile began coming back. It was infectious. Randy's anger subsided against his will and the corner of my mouth lifted slightly into a wry smile.

"You would probably enjoy it too much anyway." Randy said, dropping the ball at Tony's feet as he turned and walked back to the squad.

After practice, Randy was driving the old Chevy back home when the truck started coughing and the motor quit on him. "Shit," he cursed to himself as he coasted to the side of the road. He got out and lifted the hood. Gas poured out of a cracked fuel line with enough force to be concerned about it catching on fire. He got out the tool box from behind the seat for a pair of vice grips. As he squeezed the fuel line shut, the flow of gas stopped, but he was six miles from the ranch and it was getting dark.

With his head still under the hood he heard the sound of crunching gravel and looked up to see a brand new '62 Cadillac pull up behind the truck.

"Hey! Bartlett!" Tony Swanson yelled from the window of the Caddy. "Nice ride!"

"Great. Swanson. It just keeps getting better and better," Randy said under his breath.

"Need some help sweetheart?" Tony said with that big smile of his. Randy could tell he was enjoying this.

"Got it covered, Swanson," he lied. The last thing he wanted was help from this guy. He'd rather walk all the way back to town.

"C'mon Bartlett," Tony coaxed. "Hop in and I'll give you a lift home. Make up for the cheap shot I gave you today. Show you a little gratitude for not kicking my ass."

Randy quickly weighed out his options. Walk the eight miles back to town, the six to the ranch or get in the car with Tony Swanson. He got in the car.

Randy was not used to this kind of luxury. Air conditioning, leather seats and that new car smell engulfed him as soon as he closed the door. Swanson was beaming behind the wheel. His smile was big and genuine, so Randy allowed himself to relax a little.

"Where to Bartlett?" he asked like a well trained dog looking forward to his next command.

"Hawkins Road, 'bout six or seven miles up The Six. I'll pay you for the gas."

"Wouldn't hear of it. It's my pleasure," he said through his big perfect teeth. He hit the gas and the tires screeched when they came off the dirt and hit the hot black top. Randy figured he could endure this for the ten minutes or so it would take to get to the ranch.

After a minute or two Tony said, "Sorry about the cheap shot today, Bartlett. Really. Sometimes what I think is funny isn't too funny to other people."

"No shit," Randy said without looking at him, trying to hold on to his sour attitude.

"Guess I get it from my mom," Tony continued. "She drives people crazy with her jokes. She has a pretty heavy Italian accent and sometimes they don't translate to English too well. I've seen some people get pretty pissed at her."

"Sounds like a riot," Randy replied.

"No, she's great. People just don't get her sometimes. But I always have so I'm a big fan." The Texas landscape ticked by, one telephone pole at a time, like the second hand of a clock. "We've lived here two years now and she hasn't really connected with many people. Guess I could say the same thing."

"Stop, I'm tearin' up," Randy growled, but he regretted saying that as soon as it came out. "Sorry," he added. "I appreciate the ride. Don't mean to be a dick."

"That's okay," Tony smiled. "I know you can't help it." They stared at each other for a second then burst out laughing.

The next mile passed in silence. No surprise Tony broke it.

"So what's your story Bartlett?"

Randy took a deep breath. He wasn't used to this. Since he'd lived in Calvert all his life, everyone here already knew 'his story'. He'd never had to tell it to anyone.

"Not much to tell. My Dad and me have a cattle ranch out on Hawkins Road. It used to be part of an old cotton plantation. My grandfather passed it on to him before I was born. We've been workin' it all our lives."

"No Mom?"

Randy said "no" and Tony didn't push the subject. The sign for Lambert Road approached, indicating the halfway point to the ranch.

"My family are ranchers too," Tony said matter-of-factly, not bragging even though Randy knew the Swanson Ranch was one of the biggest in Calvert. "I don't get involved much though," Tony continued. "Not my thing. It's my Dad's dream. He was in the oil business in Houston, but ranching was always what he wanted to do."

"So what do you do?" Randy asked. He was curious what Tony's role was because all he knew was ranching. He had no knowledge of the outside world beyond the boundary wire of his ranch. His spread was the only place he'd ever wanted to be, working side by side with Hank and bringing cattle to market. It was all he'd ever wanted.

"I'm a money guy," said Tony. He kept both hands on the wheel as he talked, never taking his eyes off the road. Randy could tell he was like that in everything he did, never taking his eyes of the ball, the girl or the money, whatever was in his sights. "I like making it, I want it, and I know where to put it where it does the most good." This young guy had a calling. Make money, grow it and keep it. "My father doesn't see much beyond the ranch anymore. He has tunnel vision. The ranch is a stepping stone to where the real money is but he is blind to the possibilities. My contribution to the Swanson family is not going to be limited to four legs." Tony gripped the wheel with both hands as he talked.

"This is a serious guy," Randy thought, and before he could stop himself he began to respect Tony Swanson.

They passed the old abandoned gas station at Collier Road. The rusted Texaco sign marked four miles to the ranch. The windows were broken out and the open garage door was a cool black maw inviting rodents to spend the day in the shade.

"So what are you doing after graduation, Bartlett? What's the plan? You goin' to A&M?"

Texas A&M in College Station was where all the college bound Calvert kids were expected to go. His eyes darted in Randy's direction. He really wanted to hear the answer to this question.

"Hank and I want to rebuild the barn next year. Not goin' to college," Randy said. He thought for sure Tony would not be too impressed with his simple goals but to his surprise Tony said,

"Let me know when you want to get the materials. My Dad has a lot of pull with Harris Lumber. I think I could get your wood at a big discount."

Randy was floored by this gesture and didn't know what to say. Hank would shit if they could pull that off. The Haskell Ranch mailbox flashed by. Two miles more to go.

"I'll make you a deal, Bartlett," Tony said with the voice of a much older man. Randy sensed he was about to be asked a serious question. "If you can keep me from getting hurt this season I will do everything in my power to help you and your Dad get your place into shape next year. I don't want to show up in College Station next fall on crutches. What do you say?"

Not for the first time in this short drive Randy Bartlett recognized the strength in Tony Swanson. Clearly he meant what he said. "If I can help him, he will help me," Randy thought," and he said the only thing he *could* say.

"It's a deal."

Chapter 5

At a truck stop where the Texas Highway 6 meets Interstate 35 just outside of Waco a waitress is cleaning up the stacks of newspapers left by the truck drivers from all over Texas and beyond. Big cities. Small towns. Places she has seen and places she wants to see but never will. Her life is not what she had planned, mainly because she did not plan it at all; it just happened.

She's past her prime but still pretty and her petite figure still turns the heads of the burly truckers who whistle and flirt with her. Her once glossy blonde hair is dulling and the lines on her small face are getting deeper. Her pink uniform is stained with ketchup and bacon grease. On the left side over her heart her name is embroidered in swirly white threaded script: *June.*

As she scoops up the used newspapers she spots a familiar town paper, the Bryan-College Station Eagle. The sports section headline reads: *"Bryan High School takes on arch rival Calvert High School."* Under the headline the team photos of the Bryan High Vikings and the Calvert High Trojans show young men standing straight and looking serious in their football jerseys. She cannot help herself and reads the names, knowing what she might find. There it is. From the rear left to right, three boys over is Randall Bartlett, OG. As she stares at the picture a feeling both icy cold and burning hot at the same time pierces her heart.

June runs her red polished finger around the young man's face. He's taller than most of the other boys in the picture and larger framed. His straw blonde hair partially covers one eye. He's also one of the few smiling for the camera. How handsome and strong he looks! She wants to throw her arms around him and kiss his cheeks. She aches to hear him call her *Mom.* Her love for him has not diminished since the day she kissed him goodbye as he lay sleeping in his crib. Something wet hits the paper as she gazed upon her son's face, then again and again. Her tears turn the paper transparent and soft. She tears the picture from the paper, folds it gently, making sure not to crease her son's image, and puts it in the pocket of her food spotted apron. For the first time today the dark shadow of regret has crept into her soul as it has almost every day for the past seventeen years.

Chapter 6

Randy stepped down off the porch and walked towards the barn. How could everything have gone so wrong so fast? Hank was gone, the ranch was in shambles, and his life had no direction. Even the seven years he spent in Montana had not softened the loss of his father and his home as much as he thought it would.

He looked into his hand and realized he was still holding Hank's old lighter. He stroked the surface of the stainless steel with his thumb and felt the dents and scratches in the metal, wondering if they were put there on some remote Pacific island or just here on the ranch. Sliding the lighter back into his pocket, Randy reached for the door handle of the Chevy, which opened reluctantly as he gave it the all-too-familiar yank that allowed entry. The ashtray still had so many old butts in it that the tray hung open. Randy couldn't remember ever seeing it closed all the way unless he dumped it out himself. The keys were still in the ignition. He slid into the driver's seat through the cobwebs and dust, crossed his arms over the wheel, rested his head, and remembered that last day….

The hand painted mailbox came up on the left. 'Bartlett' was written on it in a child's handwriting. Randy had painted it for a Father's Day surprise for Hank when he was eight. Hank had acted as though his son had just painted the Mona Lisa. Randy remembered finding a small glass bottle of red paint in one of the drawers of the bathroom vanity. As he opened the bottle a strange odor wafted out and he could see a brush attached to the cap. The bottle called upon him to paint something with it and the mailbox seemed the perfect place.

The letters were a little faded now but were still clear, just as his memory of the day his father died....

The pavement of the road gave way to the dirt drive. Tony guided the Caddy towards the house. The setting sun was in their eyes and the silhouette of the barn and house were like a painting with a halo of light glowing behind it. Straight ahead were the barn and the old Case tractor that Hank had been trying to resurrect since last winter. Lying on the ground next to the tractor was Hank, motionless.

"Stop the car!" Randy screamed. Before the car stopped moving he opened the car door, jumped out, stumbled to the ground and staggered toward Hank. When he reached him, Hank was alarmingly still and lying on his side. Randy gently rolled him over so he and his father were face to face. Hank's steel blue eyes were open and alert.

"What's for supper, Randy?" Hank said with a grin."I hope it's not that God awful chicken casserole you like to make."

He smiled weakly.

"Don't worry Hank. I'll get you to the hospital. You'll appreciate my cooking after eating their food for a few days."

"Tony! Help me get him into the car!"

The fear and urgency in Randy's voice snapped Tony out of his trance and he jumped from the car to help get Hank into the back seat.

"Nearest hospital is in Bryan! Drive!" Randy yelled.

By the time they reached the hospital in Bryan Hank was still and his eyes were closed. Randy was terrified, more for himself than for Hank. "He can't leave me all alone. He just can't!" Randy worried. Throwing open the door, he rushed to the desk of the emergency room.

"My Dad is real sick!" he screamed at the nurse. "Maybe dying! Please help me! He's outside!" The nurse directed an orderly to get a gurney and they hurried to the car. Tony was standing next to the car with the doors open with eyes wide, honest concern on his face and obviously not knowing what to do next. The orderlies gently lifted Hank from the back seat, placed him on the gurney and hurried him into the hospital. Randy followed close behind. The nurses stopped him from entering the door to the ICU. He stood there staring blankly through the small window in the door until they disappeared down the hall.

Randy heard a voice behind him and turned. Tony was standing just inside the ER doorway talking on the pay phone: "No Mom. I don't know yet. He's a guy on my team. I just can't leave him here. I'm fine but I'm going to wait here in case he needs a ride somewhere. Okay, I'll call you later."

Tony hung up the phone and looked up at his friend.

"You okay, man?"

Randy didn't say anything. He just stared blankly into space. Tony sensed Randy's worry and confusion so he didn't press for an answer. He just walked over to a chair and sat down. Randy walked over to the row of chairs directly across from Tony and fell into one. He put his face in his hands to hide his fear and his tears. Tony said nothing. They waited in silence.

After what seemed like an eternity, a doctor emerged from the ICU. Randy jumped from his seat.

"How is my Dad doctor?" His voice was shaking and his eyes pleaded for good news.

"I'm very sorry, Mr. Bartlett, but your father is gone. He suffered a major cardiac event. There was not much we could do for him. There was just too much damage to the heart."

Randy stared at him in disbelief.

"Who is this guy?" Randy thought. "He's telling me my father is dead and I don't even know his name. He can't be right. This has to be a mistake!"

"Do you have someone we can call for you?" the doctor asked.

Randy just shook his head.

"I'd like to see him," Randy croaked. In reality Randy *needed* to see him. He needed proof that his father was dead. Otherwise his mind would simply deny it and he would expect Hank to walk out of there with him.

He followed the doctor into the ICU and he pulled back the curtain. Hank was laying there, eyes closed and hands at his sides. The crash cart was next to the bed. Randy could only guess what measures were taken to try and save him. He leaned over and kissed Hank's forehead. He couldn't remember ever kissing him before. What would Hank have said? The young man stood there taking in his father's quiet features for a minute. He seemed so much smaller now. Randy realized that it was Hank's character that made him such a big man, but now that was gone and this was all that was left.

Randy touched his hand and whispered, "Good bye Dad. I love you." He turned and left the room to return to the waiting area, where he felt a hand on his shoulder. Tony was standing there, eyes wet and full of pity.

"Come on Randy. Let's go to my house. My mom will know what to do."

Randy went with him silently to the car. He had nowhere else to go.

Chapter 7

The sun was riding lower over the barn. Its shadow shrouded the old truck and brought with it a cooling shade. "How long have I been sitting here?" Randy wondered. He slid out and walked back to the house. The key was where it always was. In a rusty Maxwell House coffee can under the porch, just behind the steps. He unlocked the door to a life he'd not entered in almost eight years.

Everything was covered in white sheets. This was not his doing. After Hank died he could not bring himself to come back to the house. "I know who did this," he said aloud. "She took care of everything."

What did he know of death, funerals and other details that come from a life gone so swiftly? He had been only seventeen and alone. She saw the pain and anger he felt at the loss of the only person in this world that he'd ever loved and who loved him back. So she took care of things.

The two bedroom house was built by his grandfather, a man as simple as the house he built. It had one large bedroom and one smaller, a living room and a kitchen. The bathroom was added later by Hank. The grandfather obviously saw no need, but Hank's new bride could not bear to use the outhouse, so he accommodated her by building her a bathroom with an adjacent powder room and closet. Obviously this luxurious addition was not enough to hold her here. Randy never saw him use it and he rarely used it himself. When he was ten he poked holes in a bucket, attached a water hose to it with bailing wire and hung it from the pecan tree in the yard. Hank laughed when he saw his son showering this way. He showered that way for years.

Randy's was the smaller of the two bedrooms. He pushed open the door and stepped in. His old things were as he had left them so long ago: a few small trophies that seemed much bigger when they were won, along with an assortment of ribbons, a small stack of records and a record player that Hank bought for his son when he was fourteen.

Randy was in love with Patsy Cline back then. He thought she had the voice of an angel from Heaven. Hank used to tease him about it. The boy's face would get red with embarrassment and anger but knew his father meant no harm. Once, Hank caught him staring at a picture of her on the cover of a magazine at the market. The boy found that magazine on the kitchen table the next day. Marty Robbins, Ray Price and Jim Reeves were his idols. Their pictures, torn from magazines, still clung to the wall, held on with yellowed scotch tape and tarnished brass tacks. He also had records of Kitty Wells, George Jones, even Elvis and Chuck Berry.

He pulled the cover sheet off the bed. It was just as he'd had left it, neatly made with Grandma's hand-stitched quilt protecting it, just as it had protected Randy from monsters and evil men intending to do him harm as he slept. He got down on all fours and reached under the bed. It was still there. He pulled out Grandpa's worn and battered guitar case. Hank gave it to Randy before he was even big enough to hold it. He said he never could get the hang of it and thought that maybe someday the boy might. It was just something else that Hank was right about because he took to it right away. He gave Randy a few books on how to play and some of Grandpas' old sheet music. Before long he was playing for Hank every night after supper.

Randy opened the case and as the smell of the mahogany reached his nose he was transported back. The old Gibson had quite a few dents and scratches in it, a few that he'd put there himself but mostly that's how he got it. He didn't think Grandpa was none too careful with it. Randy's father told him that Grandpa would invite a few friends over, drink beer and play well into the night.

Grandpa loved singing and playing old Mississippi Delta Blues tunes like "Kind Hearted Woman Blues," "Come On In My Kitchen," Death Letter," and "Sweet Home Chicago." Randy learned these songs and played them for his father sometimes. Hank gave him a rare smile when he did. "Hey Good Lookin" was Hank's favorite and Randy remembers playing that song over and over for his father.

Randy pulled the guitar from the case and stroked it gently. The finish was cracked and the strings were green and brown with tarnish. He never realized memories could speak so loud and strong as they were now. Images of sitting on one of the kitchen chairs and playing Grandpa's Gibson for Hank flooded his mind. He laid it gently back into its blue velvet lined coffin.

He took the few steps towards Hank's room. When he lifted the sheet he could see his things as they were on that last day. He always kept his room neat and simple. Everything was in its place. On his dresser were his comb, brush and straight razor, all lined up and ready for use. He pulled open the top drawer to find his clothes neatly folded as though they had just came from Baskin's Western Wear in Bryan were he bought all of his clothes.

In his closet hung his only suit, long out of style, and a few of his nice cowboy shirts. Sitting patiently on the closet shelf sat his two Stetsons: the clean straw rancher's hat he wore when he had business in town or when they went to church, and the black felt hat he wore to weddings and funerals. The sweat stained work hat he wore most every other day was always hung on a hook out by the kitchen door. Randy rarely saw him without it on unless they were sitting at supper. He took down the rancher's hat and put it on. It fit perfectly.

On the shelf in the far corner sat the green ammo box that held Hank's nickel plated Colt.45 semi automatic pistol, the only thing he brought back from the war. His father had told him it had saved his life in more ways than one. The box had a heavy Master Lock on the latch. Randy went back to the dresser and opened the top drawer, pulled up the liner and retrieved the key. Hank had shown him the key's hiding place when he was sixteen after a long and serious lecture on gun safety.

He unlocked the box and opened the lid. Wrapped in an oiled rag was the pistol. The slide was removed as was the magazine; they both lay wrapped at the bottom of the box. There was no ammunition; Hank never kept it with the gun, most likely for his son's sake. To this day Randy didn't know where it was kept. His father had only shown the gun to the boy a few times and Randy had fired it only twice.

Hank brought it to the kitchen table one day where Randy was doing his homework. He was thirteen and didn't even know the gun existed until then. His father asked the boy to sit and watch carefully, and, like always, he did as he was told.

"This is not a toy Randy," he said firmly." This gun can take your life and mine away in a split second. I have seen it happen with my own eyes."

He attached the slide and Randy watched as Hank added the large rounds to the clip and pushed it into the grip. It was a well rehearsed ritual he had performed a thousand times.

They went outside and Hank put an old rusty bucket in front of the hay bales. With his left hand he pulled the slide back and a bullet went into the chamber and cocked the hammer.

"Stand behind me and cover your ears, Randy." Even though he covered his ears, when Hank fired three rapid shots the noise was deafening, nothing like the .22 they used to shoot at the coyotes that bothered the cattle sometimes. That small rifle Randy could handle easily. This was something different. This was not a gun to hunt with or to scare away varmints. It was made to kill a man. He ran over and looked at the bucket they were using for target practice. It had three entry holes in the front but the back was blown out completely. Randy knew what that meant.

"Come here Randy. I want you to fire the gun." Randy did as Hank instructed. He held the gun tightly in front of him with both hands. Hank stood behind with his hands over his son's. "When I let go, Randy, I want you to count to three then fire."

His son nodded without turning around. Hank dropped his hands and the boy counted out loud.

"One, Two, Three."

When he fired he wasn't prepared for the recoil. The power of the weapon shocked him as the gun rose and nearly flew from his hands. Hank stepped in quickly and took the gun. There was blood coming from a small cut on the web of skin that went from his right thumb to his index finger. Hank examined it and said, "It's not bad Randy. I've seen much worse. It happens when the slide comes back and your hand rides too high on the grip. Happens to a lot of first timers. Even me. Now get in the truck. There's somethin' we gotta do."

Hank engaged the safety, pulled the clip, ejected the round in the chamber and slipped the bullet into his pocket. As they got in the truck, Randy's ears were still ringing from firing the pistol. Hank drove out to the east end of the ranch. There was a muddy brown water hole out there for the cattle. Most had wandered off grazing but one cow lay on the ground unable to get up. They got out of the truck and walked over to it. The cow was thrashing and mooing obviously in much pain.

"She's suffering, Randy, and we have to end it" Hank said. He guided the boy over to the cow. Randy watched as Hank replaced the clip and chambered a shell as he had before. He put the gun in Randy's hand and released the safety.

"Same as before, Randy. Count to three then fire."

Randy held the gun close to the cow's head and began his count.

"One, Two…"

Before he reached the third count Randy turned his head and Hank stopped him.

"Don't turn away Randy," he said. "Turning away just makes killin' easier. It should never be easy. It's the hardest thing a man should ever have to do. Sometimes it just has to get done." Randy started to count again. Hank was right. It was much harder to pull the trigger when you had to watch.

Chapter 8

The car was stopped. He heard a tapping on the window of the Caddy and focused on the knuckle thumping on the glass.

"Randy?" Tony said tenuously, trying to coax his friend out of the car. Randy reached for the lever but couldn't find it. Tony unlocked the car from the outside and the lock released. The door opened but the Randy just sat there. "Come on Randy. Let's go inside," Tony said. They walked to the front door.

At Tony's house, a woman stood in the doorway. The light was behind her so Randy couldn't see her face until he came close. She had thick, curly dark hair like Tony's but with wisps of gray. Her face was as smooth as a young girl's but her eyes had the quiet wisdom more fitting of a woman her age. She lifted her arms and stepped towards him. "You poor child," she whispered softly, wrapping her arms around his neck and kissing his cheek. "Come," she said, taking Randy's hand and leading him into the house.

Randy had never been in such a house before. The entry hall and living room were enormous, almost as big as the Bartlett's barn. They walked over to a group of sofas near a huge fireplace and she motioned for Randy to sit. She sat next to him, still holding his hand.

"I am Teresa Swanson, Antonio's mother."

She traded glances with Tony. Her voice was soft with an accent Randy hadn't heard before. Being raised in Texas he was used to a Mexican accent and had even heard a few Asian people speak but never this. He remembered Tony saying his mother was Italian. Her voice was like music.

"You are Randy? Yes?"

He nodded.

"I am so sorry about your father."

It sounded like she said fah-zer.

"Is there someone we can call for you? *Famiglia?* You have family?"

Randy shook his head.

"No. There is no one else. It was just Hank and me."

"Zen you must stay here wiss us until we know what to do."

She said it as though a decision needed to be made and she had to make it. "Come. Let us find you a room."

They walked through a large archway into a long hall lined with doors on both sides. It reminded Randy of a hotel he and Hank had stayed in once in Galveston on a trip to the Gulf one summer.

She stopped in front of one of the doors, opened it and switched on the light. After leading Randy into the room, she faced him, holding both of his hands.

"We will find you some clean clothes. The bathroom is there. Rest now and I will make something for you to eat."

"Thank you Ma'am but I'm not very hungry."

"You must have something to keep up your strength. I will be back soon and you will eat." She turned and left the room. Tony was still here.

"Don't try to argue with her, Bartlett. You won't win." He smiled and closed the door behind him.

As the door closed he stood motionless for a few seconds then turned to survey his surroundings. The room was large and all the furniture looked new. The bed looked bigger that his entire room at home. Randy heard the light hum of the air conditioning, far different from the loud and humid swamp cooler at the ranch, although the familiar drone of it lulled him to sleep all summer. He lay down on the large comfortable bed and closed his eyes. It had been less than two hours since his world had been turned upside down. Hank was gone along with all that everything Randy was sure of. He felt drained and alone.

A knock on the door jerked him awake. He sat up and was confused for a second. "I must have dozed off," he thought. He reached the door the same time it opened slowly.

"Randy?" a soft voice spoke from the hall. "I have food. Please, you must eat something." When the door opened Teresa was standing with a tray. "May I come in?" she asked. These small comings and goings and asking for permission to move about felt strange to Randy. He and Hank just got up and walked from one part of the house to the other without saying "please" or "may I." Randy wasn't quite sure how to respond.

"Yes, ma'am." was the only thing he could remember as being proper.

Teresa entered the room and placed the tray on the dresser.

"Just a salad and some pasta," she said. "Please try to eat." She retreated to the hall for a minute and reentered with a neat stack of clothing. "My husband is a large man like you, so these should fit nicely." As she placed the clothing on a chair she said, "Randy, I lost my father at a young age as well. The kindness of my uncle helped me get through the hard time," she added. "You too will heal as I did."

"Yes, ma'am" was all he could say to her. She gave a warm and understanding smile then closed the door behind her.

Chapter 9

Randy woke before dawn as usual but this was not a usual day. He was in a strange place and this was the first day without Hank, his first day as an orphan. He put on the clothes Tony's mother had had left. The pants were slightly large and the shirt was slightly small but not uncomfortably so. When he opened the door to his room he heard a hissing sound, as though someone were letting all the air out of a truck tire. He followed the sound through the cavernous living room and into the kitchen.

Mrs. Swanson was standing at the counter fully dressed in ranch work clothes, faded jeans, denim shirt and well worn boots. Her dark hair was pulled back in a ponytail and the look took years off her appearance.

The smell of coffee filled the air, and as she moved aside Randy saw that the hissing came from a machine on the counter top. The hissing became bubbling and when she turned around he could see she had a small pitcher of foaming milk in her hand. Her eyes widened for a second as she noticed him standing there.

"*Buongiorno* Randy," she smiled. "That is good morning in Italiano."

"Mornin' ma'am," he said sheepishly.

"Would you like a cappuccino?" she said.

"A what?" he asked.

"A coffee, like this."

She went to the stove and from a shiny little silver coffee pot she poured dark coffee into a small cup. After adding the foamy milk, she sprinkled something on top and handed Randy the cup.

"Try it."

He sat down at the breakfast table with the foamy cup. She poured herself one too and sat beside him. He brought the cup to his mouth and his nose dove into the cinnamon scented foam. It smelled wonderful and tasted fantastic, nothing like Hank's gritty cowboy coffee that he was so used to. When he brought the cup back down to the saucer she laughed.

"Here, let me," she said and brought a dishtowel to Randy's face. "You have milk foam on your nose."

She gently wiped his face as though he were a small child.

Then she looked down at her cup as though preparing her next words carefully.

"Randy, I called the funeral director in Calvert last night and discussed with him your situation and your father. I hope you don't mind but some things needed to be handled and you have no experience with such things I am sure."

"No Ma'am I don't," he said, looking away quickly to catch his emotion. Facing the wall to hide his grief, he added, "Tony was right when he told me you would know what to do. I'm much obliged Ma'am."

"*Prego*. I am glad to help." She looked at him compassionately and patted his hand.

"I also spoke with my husband about you. He sent some men to retrieve your truck from the highway and take it to your ranch. They will stay and care for your livestock until you are ready to discuss your options. He is in the barn now. We have a very important calving that is not going well so I must go now." She stood, took the last sip of coffee and started to leave.

"Mind if I come along?" Randy asked.

"*Certo siete i benvenuti*. Of course you are most welcome." They left the kitchen and went out to the barn together.

The barn was huge and modern, nothing like his old patched up shack. You could fit ten barns from the Bartlett Ranch into this one easily. They walked across the straw-lined floor and over to the calving stall. Randy and his father had no such luxury for their herd. They simply herded the 'heavies' to a makeshift corral near the barn to keep an eye on them in case there was trouble. Most times the cattle were fine by themselves. Sometimes if there were a problem with the birthing or the mother didn't take to the calf right away, they'd have to step in to help. If they didn't the calf could die.

Randy could tell the mother cow was in distress right away. She was restless and mooing constantly, getting up and laying down again. A few men with grim faces along with two big German Shepherds stood outside the stall. They were all concerned about the mother cow but did not know how to help her.

Mrs. Swanson walked up to the largest of the men. "Carl, this is Randy Bartlett, the boy I was telling you about."

"Mr. Swanson," Randy said, offering his hand.

"Nice shirt," Carl said as he shook the boy's hand firmly. "Looks better on you than it does on me." He smiled.

"I am obliged for the hospitality, sir." Randy answered as properly as he could. Hank had always taught him how to address a man of authority.

"Give them the respect they deserve." He would say. "No more and surely no less."

"How is she?" Mrs. Swanson asked.

"Not good. Something is wrong and Rodrigo is not here. He had a family emergency in Houston and had to leave last night."

"What about the vet?" Teresa pleaded.

"Out of town," was the response from Carl Swanson.

"What do we do then?" Teresa's voice was sounding desperate.

"Without Rodrigo to help with the birthing I'm not sure." Randy stepped forward.

"Mind if I have a look?" The Swansons looked at him, then each other.

"Yes. Please, if you think you can help her." Teresa said.

Randy went around to the front of the cow and brought his arm around her neck.

"Easy mama, easy girl," he said softly. Hank had always had a way with the mother cows. He could always calm them down when they were agitated and Randy had seen him get them to settle down many times. He stroked her neck and patted her side. She was huge. "Must be a big calf," he thought.

With some coaxing he got her to lie down in the loose straw. She was ready now he could tell, but something was keeping the calf from moving down the birth canal. He slowly moved to her rear stroking her and speaking softly.

"Yo, Bossy. Easy now," he said. "Some warm water and soap please," he asked one of the barn hands. Carl nodded and the man left and returned quickly. Randy rolled up his sleeves and washed his arms in the soapy water. He went to his knees behind the mother-to-be, and reaching in gently he searched for the calf.

He found the calf's front legs in the right position, feet first as though it were diving into the world. Thank God for that. As he felt around, he could tell the calf was exceptionally large, too large to pass through on its own. Randy retracted his blood soaked arm.

"The dog's choke chain." He pointed with a bloody hand. "Take it off and give it to me," he said. The barn hand removed the chain from the dog and handed it to him. Randy placed it in the soapy water, washing it thoroughly. "Rubbing alcohol and a bowl please and a heavy screwdriver," he said firmly, and all was quickly provided. He washed the chain in the alcohol placed the loop around his thumb and again entered the mother cow, chain in hand. He found the front legs of the calf once again and with some difficulty managed to loop the chain around them. He then brought out the end of the chain and slipped the screwdriver through the ring of the chain. Sitting on the floor of the barn he placed one foot on either side of the cow's rear and grasped the chain in both hands using the screwdriver as a handle. He looked as though he were rowing a boat.

"It's all in the legs!" Randy said. He could almost hear Hank's voice as he said it. He pulled with his arms and pushed with his legs for maximum leverage, just as Hank had taught him. After a few moments he felt the calf moving. The mother bellowed but she did not try to get up. He kept a slow steady pull and felt the calf coming further. As the hooves appeared, Randy heard a collective gasp from behind him. Letting go of the chain, he grabbed the hooves with his hands and pulled harder. The head appeared along with what seemed like gallons of amniotic fluid, manure and blood soaking his clothes. He wrapped his arms around the calf's neck and head. One more pull and the calf came into his lap. The mother began licking her newborn right away and it took its first breath.

Cheers and cries echoed in the barn behind Randy. As he sat there with the slick calf he looked up at the shocked and smiling faces that surrounded him. He grinned and said, "Sorry about the shirt, sir." Carl laughed loudly and hugged Teresa. The barn hands were cheering and slapping each other on the back. Randy saw tears of joy streaming down Teresa's face.

Chapter 10

"I heard you had quite a morning Bartlett," Tony said, leaning over one of Teresa's wonderful coffees. Randy had showered and borrowed more clothes from Carl. For breakfast he was eating what Teresa called a *frittata*. Not bad.

"All this before the sun came up? You sure know how to make a first impression, Randy. Wish I had been there to see it."

"You overslept, Tony." Randy said.

"No. I'm just not a 'crack of dawn' kinda guy that's all. I keep banker's hours. I need my beauty sleep."

"It ain't workin'," Randy joked, looking at him sideways as Tony choked a little on his coffee.

"Your mom is somethin' else," Randy said.

"Told ya. If a woman had balls hers would be the size of one of those bulls out there." Tony stood and refilled his cup. "She comes from tough stock. Her family in Italy are big time ranchers, have been for generations. Somewhere in the Tuscan Hills."

"What brought her here?" Randy asked.

"She came here to study at Texas A&M and get a degree in Animal Science. Her uncle expected her to bring that knowledge back to Italy and eventually take over the Conti family cattle business.

"What happened? Why didn't she go back?"

"Isn't it obvious? She met my dad."

He went on. "Dad's family was in oil, logistics mostly. Moving oil by truck, train or tanker. My grandfather was a controlling bastard and bullied dad into the business after he got his degree from Mays Business School at A&M. His major was Supply Chain

Management with a minor in Business. While he was here he became interested in the agricultural business, especially cattle ranching. It was what he really wanted to do. That was his passion but my grandfather wouldn't hear of it. No son of his was going wade ankle deep in cow shit for a living. So he pressured him into going back to Houston after he graduated to learn the family trade.

"A friend of my dad's invited him to a barbeque for the Science Department at an alumnus ranch here in Calvert. My parents met at that party and hit it off right away. They dated throughout his senior year. My mom was a junior with plans to go back to Italy after graduating.

"After my dad graduated his father forced him to move back to Houston. They had a long distance relationship for the next year while mom finished school. He worked for his father in the family business during the week and would drive out here to be with mom on the weekends. They got married after she graduated and moved to Houston. My dad promised her they would have their ranch one day. Her family didn't approve of the marriage and cut her off. It broke her heart. She didn't go back until late last year. Her uncle was sick so she finally went back home to Italy to see him.

"We lived in Houston until my grandfather passed away two years ago. My dad sold the business and bought this place with his inheritance. My grandfather must have rolled over in his grave." Tony smiled a little when he said this. He obviously wasn't close with his grandfather.

"That's our family story, Bartlett. My folks are finally realizing their dream and I'm just along for the ride."

Chapter 11

Randy returned to the porch with its peeling paint and looked out from his old home. "What am I doing back here?" he thought. "Did I think I could pick up where I left off? Just start over like the last eight years didn't happen?" No. He wasn't the same person. "Take one step at a time Randy," he told himself.

Three days ago Randy had no idea he would be sitting on this porch again. That's when he got the phone call from Tony asking him to come back. Something was happening with Teresa. She was in trouble and needed his help. That's all he would say for now.

"Just come home, Brother," was all he said, so Randy left Montana the next morning and drove to Texas. If Teresa needed him, he couldn't say no. He owed her.

He stepped down from the porch and walked over to the beat-up Ford ranch truck he'd driven from Montana. As he got in he glanced over his shoulder at the house. Would he ever come back? He wasn't sure. For now the Gibson and Hank's Stetsons were all he wanted to take with him. He closed the front door, got into the Ford and headed down the driveway, stopping at the mailbox. "Bartlett," it said, barely legible but still there. His old life was here in Calvert, but his new life was still uncertain. He drove over to see Tony for the first time in seven years.

As he pulled up to the Swanson place the first thing he noticed was the lack of activity, only a few head of cattle grazing and a couple of horses romping in the big corral by the barn. "Where is everybody?" he wondered out loud. After coming up through the big circular driveway to the house, he got out of the truck and walked up to the front door. He was about to ring the bell when the door opened. It was Tony, in a wheel chair and looking like hell. Randy was shocked and speechless. Tony's hair was long and greasy. He had an unkempt beard and was shirtless. His skin color was pallid and gray like that of an old man. This was the first time Randy had seen him since the accident.

"Long time no see, Brother," he said. The smell of booze and body odor hit Randy like a slap to the face.

"What's the matter Randy? Have I really changed that much?"

Randy recognized the sarcastic tone as pure Tony, but the bitterness was new. He rolled backward as he spoke and Randy stepped forward into the house.

"Pretty quiet out there, Tony," he said, following his old friend into the house. Randy trailed behind as the chair glided silently across the stone floor except for the occasional squeak of the tires.

"I'm afraid the old homestead just ain't what it used to be, Randy," he said as he continued to roll forward without looking back at Randy.

"Where is Teresa?" Randy asked.

"Italy."

He said it like she was on a day trip shopping in Houston. "She's been gone a year now."

Tony finally reached his objective, the bar near the big fireplace. Randy heard ice hitting a glass and the sound of a drink being poured, a big one. He raised his voice slightly.

"If she is in Italy why the hell did you call me to come back here?"

"Long story, Bro. Want a drink?"

Randy shook his head.

"Suit yourself." He took a long pull from his glass.

"What's going on Tony?" Randy demanded.

"A lot has happened since you split, Bro. After this happened." He lifted his pajamas to reveal his shrunken, atrophied legs then let them back down. "Mom and I had some differences." He took another drink from his glass. "She felt I needed to get on with life. Make the most of it. What life? This isn't living!" He threw his glass at the fireplace and shards sprayed over the room.

"I'm sorry, Tony." Randy said softly. "The accident wasn't your fault. I'm sorry this happened to you. You don't know how many times I wished it were me instead of you that night, but I can't change what happened to you and your father." He could feel the tears burning as the memories of that terrible night rushed in. "I know you blame me and I can't help that. I know that if I had never come here the accident might never have happened. I live with that every day."

"I bleed for you, Bro." he slurred. "Oh, that's right. I already have." He returned to the bar to pour himself another drink.

Randy turned and headed for the door.

"That's right, Randy. Run away! That's what you're good at!" Tony screamed. "What's the matter, Brother? Can't stand the sight of your own handy work?!"

Randy kept walking out the door and headed for the truck. He brought his fists down on the hood.

"Damn him! I wish I could have made him understand what the guilt did to *me* and to *my* life." Randy knew he wasn't directly to blame, but his coming there did set things in motion that left the Swanson family shattered....

Chapter 12

There was a soft knock on the door. Teresa entered the room with an apology.

"Randy? I do not wish to disturb you while you are resting but Carl asked me to see if you have a minute to talk. Do you?"

"Sure Ma'am. Now is just fine." She led him to the back of the house and stopped at a set of large double doors.

"Carl is waiting for us in his office." She pushed open the double doors and they stepped into the room. Carl Swanson was at his big modern desk and stood as they entered.

"Have a seat, Randy. Let's talk for a minute." He gestured to an overstuffed chair in front of his desk. Teresa went around and stood behind Carl placing her small hands on her husband's broad shoulders.

"That was quite a show you put on this morning, son. We were all very impressed with your skills. You have no idea what that calf means to us." He was smiling broadly.

"I had a good teacher," Randy replied.

"Yes, your father. He must have been quite a man."

"Yes, he sure was. Taught me everything I know," Randy said, looking at his shoes as he spoke.

"I'm sorry for your loss Randy. You're fortunate to have had a father like that. Believe me, I know."

"Thank you, sir."

He paused a moment then said, "My wife tells me you have no other family and a ranch that you can't run on your own." Randy looked at him and waited for him to continue. "We want to have you stay on here with us if you would like to. At least until the end of the school year and you can make some decisions. We could incorporate your herd into ours and shut down your ranch for the time being. Then, when you're ready you can decide what you want to do. What do you think about that idea?

"That's very kind of you both," he said. "I don't know what to say."

Then Teresa smiled and said.

"Just say yes, Randy."

"Thank you. I'd like that." He paused then and said, "But I will need to pull my own weight. I'd like to help with the ranch if you'll let me." Carl Swanson stood and reached out his hand and Randy took it.

"We can always use a good man around here."

"*Benvenuti nella vostra nuova casa* Randy. Welcome to your new home." Teresa said then came around the desk gave him a hug and kissed both cheeks. So much hugging and kissing! This family was nothing like anything he'd known before.

Two days later Randy found himself standing in the church cemetery in Calvert, wearing one of Carl Swanson's black suits and holding a neatly folded American flag. The service was mercifully short. Hank was not a very social man, so he had few friends even though he'd lived there all of his life. Mostly there were men who respected Hank as a good rancher and as a man who did honest business with the local tradesmen with few but always kind words.

There was also Marge Williams, the waitress at Lorretta's Café. She's had a crush on Hank as long as Randy could remember. He'd never seen Hank pay for coffee as long as she was serving it. At the funeral, she wept as much for herself as she did for Hank. He was perhaps her last hope to escape her destiny of becoming an Old Maid.

One by one the mourners left the cemetery, leaving only Randy, Tony and Teresa. The young man was frozen in the moment. He knew that if he turned and walked away he'd be letting go of the man who meant everything to him in this world. Randy wasn't ready. To let go was to face the fact that he was truly alone. He felt a strong hand on his shoulder and a smaller hand slipping into his palm.

"Come Randy let us go home," Teresa said softly.

That afternoon when he got back to the Swanson place there was a box on his bed with a note:

Randy,

These are the things your father had with him at the hospital. I thought you would want them.

Love Teresa.

He opened the lid of the box to find the last personal possessions of Hank Bartlett: wallet, belt and buckle; boots; sweat stained Stetson; and trusty Zippo lighter. Randy closed the box and wept quietly.

Chapter 13

"Is Tony right?" Randy wondered. "Is running away really what I'm good at?" He walked towards the barn to cool off and think. Should he just head back to Montana and leave the Swansons alone forever, or should he stay and see how he could help the family that had done so much for him not so long ago?

As he entered the huge barn he could see that little had gone on here for some time. Did the Swansons just give up? Randy needed to know and Tony had the answers.

When he got back to the house he found Tony slumped in his chair passed out. He was not going to like what Randy had to do next.

"What the fuck?!" Tony screamed as the water rushed over him. While he was passed out, Randy had wheeled him into the large master bath, removed his soiled pajamas, placed him on the floor of the big walk-in shower, and turned on the water. Tony snapped awake immediately when the water hit him.

"If you want to smell like livestock I'll treat you like livestock, Tony. This is how we get the hogs ready to show at the fair back in Montana." He grabbed a bottle of shampoo and squirted the blue soap all over him and began scrubbing him down with a wash cloth. Tony swung his arms wildly trying to get away, but Randy held him down with one hand and scrubbed him with the other.

"You son of a bitch! Let me up you fucking coward!"

"Sticks and stones, Swanson. Don't make me have to use the toilet brush," Randy warned. Tony continued to struggle so Randy popped his friend in the nose at about half speed. A little blood was mixing with the water, making the damage look worse than it really was. Tony stopped fighting him then and looked up, defeated. Blood and blue soap mixed together, making purple suds on his skin.

"Big man, beating up on a handicapped guy." Tony growled, "What's next, Bartlett? Small children and puppies?" he snarled as blood ran from his nose. Randy waved a razor in his face.

"I would hold very still if I were you Tony. I'd hate for you to lose something you're fond of."

The shaving finished without incident.

After the shower, Randy got Tony into some clean clothes and wheeled him into the kitchen to see what he could find to feed him. He scrounged up some cheese, eggs, a few potatoes, some dried herbs and an onion—all he needed to make one of Teresa's frittatas.

"What are you now, my nursemaid?" Tony squawked with that famous attitude of his.

"No, I'm not your nursemaid, Tony. I'm just your brother." Tony glared at Randy while he cooked.

When the food was ready, he rolled Tony over to the breakfast table and placed the food in front of him. To Randy's surprise he dug in right away. It must have been days since he'd last eaten.

"Been a long time since I have had one of these," he said with his mouth full. "You must have been paying attention when Mom tried to teach you how to make them."

"I do try," Randy said as he watched Tony wolf down his meal.

After he had eaten, Randy took him back to the living room and sat on one of the big couches as he faced his brother.

"Okay, Tony, talk to me."

Tony wheeled toward the bar, but Randy grabbed his chair.

"No booze." Randy said. "What happened here Tony? Why is Teresa in Italy and what kind of trouble is she in?"

Chapter 14

A few days after Hank's funeral, Randy decided that he needed to get back to work. He was spending too much time with his thoughts and was feeling a little guilty about his new luxurious surroundings.

"But Randy. Why do you wish to sleep in the bunkhouse?" Teresa asked, "Is your room not comfortable?"

"A little too comfortable ma'am" he answered. "I'd like to get to know the ranch and see where I best fit in."

"Do not forget you still have school and football," Teresa reminded him.

"I know and I will finish school," he said. "I also promised Tony that I wouldn't let him get hurt on the field and I intend to keep my word. We wouldn't want him limping off to college would we?"

She kissed him on the cheek and said, "I will talk with the foreman and let him know you will be coming over but I will miss our morning cappuccinos."

"I'm not missin' those, ma'am. I'm afraid I'm hooked."

Earl Perkins was the foreman at the Swanson Ranch. He had worked for the previous owner almost ten years before Carl Swanson bought the place two years ago. He was old school cowboy but was getting on in years so giving orders instead of doing the heavy lifting suited him just fine.

"Most of the men go home every night but a few stay over, especially if their wives get surly and kick 'em out." Earl laughed at this. "As you can see the bunkhouse is set up with small private rooms. The showers and toilets are there and we even have a decent kitchen." He was giving Randy the ten-cent tour. "Take any empty room you like. There's plenty. Linens are washed every week and the laundry room is on the other side of the kitchen. Make yourself at home, Randy." This was more like it. Simple, neat and clean. More of what he was used to. It felt more like home here.

After Randy got settled he found Earl again.

"How's that new red calf?" he asked. "Everything okay?"

"Yeah, he's fine. He shore was a big one though, wasn't he?"

Randy nodded and said, "He must have been over eighty pounds."

"More like ninety."

Randy whistled at this. "No wonder the mother had such a hard time pushing him out."

"Getting bigger by the day too. Bet he's well over a hundred already," Earl said.

"Damn!" Randy said. "What's his stock?"

"Not rightly sure. Mother was an Angus, I know that much. Don't know about the stud. You should ax' Mr. Swanson. He's taken a special interest in that calf. So has the Missus."

Randy felt good getting back into a routine. He would ride to school with Tony every day and afterward they had football practice. By this time everyone knew about Hank but few said anything. He found himself spending more time with Tony. Unfortunately, that meant he had to run interference for his smartass friend when he pissed someone off, which was pretty often. He either had to stop a fight or finish one. On the plus side the girls loved Tony and there were always pretty girls around. A few got tired of waiting for him and

Randy was the next best thing. He didn't mind being second choice at all. Any female attention was good attention as far as he was concerned.

When he wasn't at school or practice Randy worked on the ranch. He did anything he was asked to do and more. The Swansons paid him working wages too and he saved almost every penny. He wasn't sure what he was saving for but everything else was provided and he had inherited Hank's frugality.

Earl asked him to cut some of the new calves and their mothers out to the more open part of the ranch. If they stayed huddled together too long they could transmit disease. On the pasture they had to be checked daily to be sure they got enough to eat and stayed healthy. Randy saddled up a good horse and started bringing them out a pair at a time.

Then he noticed the big calf that he'd helped bring into the world. It was with its mother grazing. Something was different about it besides being larger than normal. Its red coloring was fading to white with a darker stripe along the back and its skin and nose were black. The calf's rump and thighs seemed a bit out of proportion to the rest of his body, bigger and fuller than the Brahman or Angus that Randy was used too. Its legs appeared oddly longer too. He remembered Earl told him the Swansons had a special interest in the calf so he decided to ask them about it later at supper.

One thing about the Swansons, they ate well. Teresa was a remarkable cook and Randy ate food that he was sure he never would've tried had he not come here. A far cry from Hank's meat and potatoes or chili and corn bread, these dishes had names he could barely pronounce: *risotto, ravioli, minestrone, ribollita, gnocchi, fagoli, tortellini, pesto, cannelloni, pappardelle, linguine, pomodori, prosciutto*. Such words had no meaning until he tasted Teresa's cooking. She served vegetables he'd never eaten before, like artichokes, eggplant and zucchini, and he tried familiar food cooked in ways he couldn't imagine. Chicken, pork, beef or fish were prepared very differently from what he'd known, but they were so simple and delicious.

Hank and Randy didn't eat much cheese but it was a staple here. Teresa could turn a small piece of cheese, a few vegetables and some pasta or rice into a beautiful meal. The cheeses had names like *ricotta, parmigiano, romano, pecorino, fontina, or mozzarella*. Every meal was an adventure of discovery.

Until he came to the Swanson home the closest he ever got to Italian food was a can of Chef Boyardee Spaghetti-O's or the occasional pizza. As for pizza, Teresa had a brick oven just outside the back door of the kitchen and she made them out there. The *"forno"* as she called it, brought forth the most incredible pizzas and breads. She taught him to start the fire and soon it became Randy's responsibility to ready the oven. In Italy she'd used fallen wood from the olive trees for the oven but here in Texas mesquite did quite nicely. The hot fire produced a crispy, slightly charred crust like no pizza Randy had ever tasted.

Teresa also introduced him to Chianti, a deep red fruity wine from her homeland in Tuscany. They had a glass of it with almost every evening meal.

"My family has a small winery in Montepulciano. They grow the Sangiovese grape which is the main grape for Chianti. Some of the best wines in Italy are produced in that region," she said with pride.

Maybe the biggest discovery for Randy was olive oil. Never had Randy tasted this greenish, fruity, buttery and nutty nectar, nor had seen it used in so many dishes. Often before dinner Teresa would put out some freshly baked bread with a plate of olive oil and dark vinegar with crushed garlic. Randy would devour the plate before realizing no one else had any. They would laugh at him and protest until Teresa put out more. She affectionately scolded him for being such a *Cinghiale*, a big piggish boar and hit him with her wooden spoon.

That night as they were finishing dinner, Randy turned to Carl and said, "Sir, I've been wondering about the calf I helped with that first night. It seems so different from the others." He went on to describe the calf and the curious way it was changing color from red to white with its odd black skin. He noted its distinct and different shape.

He could see Carl's eyes glancing at Teresa as he spoke of the calf. When he saw her eyes dart from Carl back to Randy, he knew they were sharing a secret. Tony could see this too.

"What?" he asked.

Teresa nodded to Carl. He took a sip of wine and said, "That calf is very special to us Randy. The first of his kind but we hope the first of many. Now what we are about to tell you must remain at this table. Understand? Tony? Randy?"

They both nodded.

Carl began.

"In Italy there is a breed of cattle called The Chianina, Kee-ah-neen-a. It is one of the oldest breeds in the world. It goes back to the days before the Roman Empire and even long before that. Well over 2000 years. Back then they were work animals used mainly to pull carts and plows like we used mule teams here. They are among the largest and the strongest cattle ever in history. There have been some that have reached over six feet tall and weighed almost 4000 pounds!"

"This can't be true," Randy thought. True the calf was big, maybe the biggest he'd ever seen at his age, but could it really get that big?

Carl continued, "The beef steak in Italy from this breed is famous the world over. It's a T-bone they call *Bistecca Fiorentina* or Florentine Steak. It's very rare outside of Italy. One cut of this huge steak can feed two or even three people. The cut is three inches thick. It is tender, juicy, low in fat and has a very clean flavor. Simply grilled over an open fire it may be the best tasting steak in the whole world.

"When Teresa and I first met in school she told me the history of the Chianina. Her family has been raising and breeding them for almost 100 years in her home near Siena in Tuscany. The cattle are range fed, and the Conti Family had some of the largest land holdings in the area. Since the Chianina are no longer needed as work animals and are poor milk producers, they're strictly raised for meat and there are now not many more than 10,000 head in all of Italy. The Conti Family has almost a third that number on their ranch alone and they are among the finest specimens in the country.

"Since the breed is so drought tolerant, grows so fast and doesn't have a mean bone in its body it's perfectly suited for the Texas climate and it's easy to raise. So Teresa and I decided years ago when we were still in school that someday we would bring the Chianina here to Texas and breed them with our Angus and Brahman. We wanted to create a cross breed that we could raise here in Calvert. A whole new breed of cattle never before seen that would be well suited for Texas. After that we we'd bring it to other parts of the U.S., like California, Wyoming and Montana."

"Here is the catch." He looked at Tony and Randy, and then paused for a moment. "The breeding of the Chianina has been very tightly controlled since the 1930's. The *Ministero di Agricoltura e Forestre*, the Ministry of Agriculture and Forestry tracks and registers the stock. But the most difficult part is a group of very powerful ranching families in Tuscany who have been maintaining a herd book for over 100 years. There are those in this society that do not want the Chianina to leave Italy and want to control the breed completely. They fear that losing control of the breeding rights would endanger the purity of the breed and the *Societa degli Agricltori Valdichiana,* the Agricultural Society of the Chiana Valley, would be lost along with their power."

"They also work together to keep the number of head low. That way they can control the price of the beef. This keeps the supply low and the demand high so they can always get top dollar for their cattle, even dictating which butchers are allowed to sell the meat and which ones aren't. There are men in this society who'll stop at nothing to prevent the loss of this control. Millions of dollars are at stake. No pun intended."

We all chuckled and Carl received a playful slap from Teresa for his bad joke.

Tony asked the obvious question.

"So if the breed is so controlled, how is it we have a Chianina half breed running around the ranch?

Chapter 15

Siena, Italy — One Year Earlier

It had been many years since Vincenzo Conti had seen his cousin Teresa. She went off to America to study and was to return to help Zio Pietro manage the ranch. Now Uncle Pietro was getting old and was not in good health. He too had wished Teresa would return to take her place as Pietro's successor as he had no sons. Instead she chose to stay in America and marry a man from Texas. Saddened by her decision Pietro expressed it by lashing out in anger. He cursed her and vowed never to speak of her again. After almost twenty years he had kept his word.

Vincenzo made no such vow. He and Teresa grew up together because their mothers were very close sisters. They were raised more like siblings than cousins. Together they made mischief and were often scolded for the trouble they would get into. They would climb the olive trees and help with the autumn harvest. They played house in the ruins of the old stone farmhouse near the pond. Her father and Enzo's were *butteros,* cowboys on the Conti ranch. When Teresa's father died, Zio Pietro took her and her mother in. They grew even closer then. He held her while she cried for her father and vowed to be her friend always. Later, when her mother passed away, she felt so alone and Vincenzo comforted her. There was a bond between them that could not be broken.

As Vincenzo grew into a young man he too came to work on the Conti ranch as a *buttero* himself. He tended to the cattle as they roamed the pastures and kept watch over the mother cows that were ready to give birth or tended to calves that needed help. He also assisted with the breeding, either naturally by herding cows that were ready to the selected bulls or by insemination to insure the birth of a selected pure bred Chianina calf. The lineage was well documented in the *Societa degli Agricoltori della Valdichiana* herd book and the bloodlines could be traced back one hundred years. Vincenzo was proud of this tradition and took his job very seriously.

After Teresa decided to stay and marry the American they had stayed in contact. They wrote to each other often, exchanged photos and even spoke on the telephone a few times a year, never telling Zio Pietro. This was one of those times.

"Teresa! Como stai? Mi manchi cosi tano!" he yelled into the telephone.

"I miss you too Enzo! I am fine. How is *Zio*, Uncle Pietro?"

"Not well I am afraid, Teresa." Enzo said sadly. "The *medico* says he has diabetes and must take better care but he does not listen. He needs a strong hand to force him. There is no one as strong as you Teresa. He will listen to no one else. Without you I am afraid he will not last. Can you come?"

"He will not see me, Enzo. What can I do if he will not allow me to come home?" she says.

"He will once he sees your face, Teresa. I know it," Enzo assured her. "His anger will melt as a candle in the Cattedrale di Santa Maria del Fiore as soon as you walk in the door. I have seen it in my dreams. *Si prega,* Teresa! Please come home!" Enzo pleaded.

Teresa hung up the phone, wiped her tears and went out into the late night air. Walking past the house and towards the barn, she saw Carl standing alone in the big doorway. He was just staring into the barn lost in thought. She often caught Carl day dreaming. When they lived in Houston he would dream of the ranch they would one day have together and she would see him with that same faraway look planning his escape to someday. Now after all this time, the ranch was finally theirs and he would do almost anything to make it a success. He would never let his dream die.

"Buonasera il mio amore. Good evening my love,"* she said softly as she wrapped her arms around him from behind. He smiled and turned.

"I never get tired of hearing that." As he reached his hands to her face to kiss her he saw that she had been crying.

"What is it? What's wrong?" he said with worry in his voice.

"It is my Uncle Pietro. He is not well and I do not know what to do." She buried her face in Carl's chest. Between sobs she told him what Enzo had said.

"You must go to him Teresa," Carl said.

The next morning Carl drove Teresa to the airport in Houston.

"What if he will not see me? Teresa asked Carl.

"All you can do is try *mio tesoro*, my darling." Carl smiled." See? I have been paying attention." Teresa laid her head on his shoulder as he drove.

Chapter 16

Teresa landed at the airport in Rome and phoned Carl to let him know she had arrived safely and picked up her rental car, a small red Fiat 500. Leaving the city, she realized that she had not traveled these roads for nearly twenty years but still she needed no map to guide her. The hill towns between Rome and Siena had been here for centuries. Twenty years meant little to those old stone walls. She passed the familiar towns with their ancient church steeples and towers rising above the red tiled rooftops.

The two hour drive to Siena passed quickly. She was excited to be home but also terrified of what lay ahead in the presence of her uncle. She would find Enzo first. "At least he will be sure to welcome me home," she said to herself. Nearing the city she could see the Torre del Maggia, one of the tallest medieval towers in all of Italy and beside it the Duomo. How long it had been since she has seen that incredible skyline. How she had taken the beauty of this city for granted when she saw it almost every day so many years ago.

She did not enter the city. Instead she took the roads that led into the surrounding countryside. The rolling patchwork hills of Tuscany appeared perfectly landscaped but no gardener could have created this beauty. Centuries of caring for the land, coaxing the soil to bring forth the bounties of what lie just beneath the surface made this topography. Sunflowers were just reaching full bloom and the hills are overwhelmed with the huge yellow flowers. There was not room for a single blossom more. The hay had been rolled and the huge round bales dotted the hillsides. Hectares of olive trees, heavy with fruit, basked in the summer sun.

She turned off the paved road and continued on through the valley. Guided more from memory than by sight she came to the drive that led to Pierto Conti's villa and stopped the Fiat just short of the entry gate. Her heart ached for home but she was not yet ready to face him. She stepped on the gas pedal and the tires of the Fiat spun in the dust and gravel. She was excited to see Enzo and full of love for this place, her childhood home.

Enzo lived in a small farmhouse on the Conti estate as did many of the families that worked for Zio Pietro. Although Teresa had never been to his home since he had lived there she still knew it well. Many of these farmhouses had stood for three hundred years or more so the families came and went but the houses remained. When Teresa was a child the house was occupied by the groundskeeper and his wife. Enzo and she would follow the poor man, pretending to help, but only getting in the way while he went about his duties. Eventually he would tire of the children and he would bring them home so his wife could distract the little ones with almond cookies and fresh cold milk as he sneaked away to get his work done.

She drove up to the same house decades later, but it was unchanged. Time moves slowly in Toscana. She stopped the car, opened the door, and stepped out into her past. Smiling, then laughing, then crying, Vincenzo emerged from the heavy old weathered front door. She ran to him and they held each other, tears of joy running down their faces.

"Teresa! I cannot believe my eyes! *Sei ancora cosi bella.* You are still so beautiful!" Enzo shouted.

"*E tu sei acora un bugiardo.* And you are still such a liar!" she shouted in return.

She had never met Enzo's family: his wife Sofia; daughter Marcella, sixteen; and the youngest his son Sergio, thirteen. Marcella was movie-star gorgeous, with long, thick, black hair and bright blue eyes. Sergio was small and thick like Enzo with an Italian profile that looked as though it should be chiseled into marble. Sofia was warm and soft spoken.

"It is wonderful to finally meet you Teresa. Enzo speaks of you so often I feel as though I know you already," Sofia said.

"Then you and I must have a long talk because I am sure he has not told you a word of truth." They all laughed at this.

Marcella asked quietly, "Zia Teresa? I am studying my English in school. Would you practice speaking with me? I want very much to go to America one day and wish to be fluent before I do."

"*Certo cara.* Of course darling. Not only will I help you with your English but I will talk with your parents about you coming to our ranch in Texas for a visit." Marcella was clearly elated.

"Oh thank you Zia Teresa. Thank you so much!" She was rewarded with a hug from her newfound favorite niece.

Enzo and Teresa walked the olive orchards of their childhood, hand in hand as they had when they were young.

"Please tell me Enzo, how is Zio Pietro managing?" she asked.

"Teresa, you know how Pietro has run everything himself for all these years. In his mind no one can do the job the way he feels it should be done. Many of us have tried to take some of the responsibilities from his shoulders but he will have none of it. Every detail must pass through his hands.

"Now that his health is failing there is no one who knows enough to take over the ranch even if he would allow it. Important decisions are not being made, supplies are not getting purchased and the workers are not getting paid when they should. Many have left frustrated and have gone to work for other families. You cannot blame them, for they must feed their own children. We now have half the number of cattle as we had only two years ago and even that number continues to fall. If this goes on soon there will be nothing left to save. Yet he still does not see and refuses help."

He stopped and turned to her. "You are his only hope Teresa. He has always trusted you even when you two disagreed and fought. He has not spoken to you all of these years because of his guilt and stubborn pride. But I know he regrets your lost relationship. He has missed you desperately and will trust no one for fear they would leave him as well. You must try to convince him to accept help and to take care of his health."

"There is more." Enzo took a breath and continued. "The other ranching families are aware of Pietros failing health and some see this as an opportunity to finally take control of the lands they have coveted for so many years. They are luring even the most loyal workers away with higher pay and are conspiring to do whatever they can to interfere with the Conti business dealings. If Pietro loses his lands it is they who have much to gain." Enzo looked her in the eyes and spoke ominously. "Listen to me now Teresa. Some of these men are very dangerous. They have hurt, perhaps even killed people that stand in the way of what they want."

Chapter 17

Teresa stood at the front door of Pietro's villa. This large stone house had stood for centuries perched on a hilltop overlooking the valley, with views of the mountains beyond. It reminded her of Pietro himself, strong and unyielding. It withstood weather and war, famine and drought, and still its strength was undiminished. She reached for the big iron ring on the door and let it rise and fall three times. The sound echoed through the house. She heard the heavy bolt slide away and the door opened.

The familiar face before her was that of Marta De Rosa, Pietro's loyal housekeeper. To call her that did her a great injustice, for she was much more. She had seen to Pietro's needs for over forty years and to the needs of the rest of the Conti family as well. She cared for him in the dark days following the death of his wife so many years ago. She had seen much sadness and joy in this house.

Marta had nursed Teresa through the measles, the chicken pox and countless colds. She stayed by her bedside when Teresa fell from a horse and broke her arm trying to prove to Zio Pietro that she too could be a *buttero* like her father. Teresa called the old woman *Nonna*, for she was the only grandmother Teresa had ever known.

"*Teresa! Lode a Dio!* Praise God!" Marta cried. She wrapped her arms around Teresa with her perfume of freshly baked bread. Marta kissed both sides of Teresa's face and stepped back, beaming.

"I cannot believe my eyes! Let me look at you."

Her eyes were wet and her smile was big and welcoming. "It has been far too long, Teresa," Marta said. "Your Zio Pietro is very sick and needs his *famiglia*."

"Yes *Nonna*, I have heard. Enzo called me a few days ago to tell me. I have come with the hope that he will see me. Do you think he will?"

"If he does not I will beat him with my broom until he does." She said this while shaking her small fist in the air. "Come. Let us go upstairs to his room. This will be quite a surprise." She raised her eyebrows and gave a huge gap toothed grin.

As she climbed the immense stone staircase Teresa had the urge to run back to her rental car and head straight for the airport, but she had come too far for that. Besides if Pietro needed her as much as everyone was saying then she must try.

Marta said, "You go ahead *cara*. I will not be far away if you need me." Marta squeezed Teresa's hand and disappeared down the hall.

As Teresa slowly pushed Pietro's door open, she saw him sitting up in bed asleep. His ledgers and paper work were spread out over the covers. Even while sick he continued to work. How old and frail he looked. She stepped quietly into the room and stood at the foot of the bed.

"Zio," she called to him softly. His eyes fluttered awake and he looked up at her, squinting as though he did not believe what his eyes are telling him.

"*E 'un sogno?* Is this a dream?" he whispered.

"No *Zio*. It is Teresa. I have come to beg your forgiveness for hurting you, and to help you get well." Tears ran down her face as she spoke. Pietro turned away, for he too was crying. "I have missed you so very much Zio," Teresa continued. "I have been too long from home. Please. Have I not been punished enough?" She begged him.

Finally Pietro turned to her without saying a word, for he could not speak through his tears, and he just opened his arms. She hurried around the bed and fell into them. He wrapped his arms around her and said only, "*Benvenuti a casa mia figlia!* Welcome home my daughter!"

At long last she was home.

They spent the next hour talking quietly and getting to know one another again. She did not want to discuss the business of the ranch, only Pietro's health and what she could do to help him get well.

When he once again fell asleep she gathered his papers and took them downstairs to the study. Marta had the name and number of Pietro's doctor. "First things first," she thought. She would speak to the *medico* right away and get familiar with Pietro's condition. Then she would attend to business.

The next afternoon after visiting the doctor in Siena, she had a clear understanding of what was needed. Pietro's diet must be strictly controlled and he must take his medication regularly. He must not work and he must rest. Poor Marta had not been able to do this alone, but together she and Teresa would. Pietro was stubborn but she would find a way. She must. Marta and she would plan how to care for him so that he could regain his strength. But from now on he must accept the fact that he would no longer run the ranch alone. The next step would be to straighten out his affairs. Teresa would need Enzo's help now and after she returned home. He was the only one who could be trusted to take on this responsibility.

Teresa planned to meet with Pietro's *avvocato*, his lawyer. She would need a *procura*, power of attorney, to make decisions for Pietro. The future of the Conti Ranch was at stake and she would not let it die.

Chapter 18

Over the next two weeks Teresa worked to stabilize the ranch. She paid off old debts and brought back some of the workers that had left. The people of the area learned of her return and many came by to pay their respects and to inquire about Pietro. Under Teresa's guidance the old man's strength was slowly returning. One afternoon he called her to his beside.

"Cara," he said." Please sit with me *un momento."*

She sat and held his hand.

"I am so happy that you have come home, Teresa, and I know, too, that soon you must return to your *famiglia* in America."

"Yes *Zio* but not right away, for there is much to be done. We shall need to sell some our cattle to raise funds. It is also time for the breeding so that we may rebuild the stock. Enzo is handling this. He is a very capable and loyal man Zio, and you must trust him."

"I know you are right Teresa. I have been a foolish old man. I am tired and it is time for *sangue nuovo*, new blood. You have shown me this." He squeezed her hand weakly.

"There are some things you need to hear about our cattle that few others know. I tell you this now because there are those that *do* know and may stop at nothing to take this place from our family. You know the high quality of our stock, but you do not know how it came to be so. I have done some things for which I am not proud, Teresa, and you must hear them."

"What is it *Zio*? What could be so *terribile?*

Pietro began.

"It has been almost eight years now; it was 1955 and I was on my way to Arezzo for the National Chianina Show. With me were three of my best animals, one bull and two cows that were *open*, in heat, for that was when I could get the best price for them. I was to auction them off to the highest bidder and hoping to get a good price so that I could purchase a new prized stud I sorely needed. Our stock was weakening with smaller animals so we needed new blood.

"I got too late of a start and decided to stop for the night and leave early the next morning. Just outside of Castlenuovo Beradenga is the small village of San Gusme."

"Yes I remember it," Teresa said. "You and I would stop there to get me a *gelato* on our trips to Florence when I was a child."

"Yes, that is the place. There is a small inn just inside the village walls with a bar and a small restaurant. I know the innkeeper Carlo Santoro well and knew he would always find room for me there…."

Chapter 19

"Pietro! So good to see you!" the innkeeper said with a welcoming smile.

"Carlo! My old friend! How is your wife?"

"As mean and ugly as ever, Pietro, but she cooks so well I could never leave her!" We laughed at this joke. His wife Zita is a lovely woman with an easy temperament.

"I hope you have room for me tonight, Carlo. I am on my way to Arezzo for the show and am too tired to go on."

"For you, Pietro, of course. Besides, we only have two other guests. They too are going to Arezzo. They have been in the restaurant all night drinking grappa and are *molto ubriaco*, very drunk. Go and sit. I will bring you something to eat."

"Grazie, Carlo."

As I sat at a table one of the men called to me and rose to his feet. His words were slurred and he was unsteady.

"I heard you say you were going the show in Arezzo tomorrow as are we," he told me. I looked over at his friend, leaning his head against the wall, asleep.

"It appears your friend is done for the night," I said.

"It appears so. He cannot hold his grappa as well as I. Funny thing, though. He is supposed to be my guard." He stepped over to the sleeping man and lifted his jacket, showing me his shoulder holster and pistol.

"And why is it that you require an armed guard?" I asked. Dropping down into his chair again, the stranger poured the last of the grappa bottle into his glass.

"It is not I that needs guarding," he said, "but it is Donetto he must watch over."

"And who is Donetto?" I asked.

"Only the finest bull in all of Italy!" the man slurred. "He stands almost two meters tall and weighs almost 2000 kilos! He is in the truck outside as we speak." The man downed the grappa in one gulp and wiped his mouth with the back of his hand, something he had done many times this evening I was sure. "He is sure to take home the prize at this year's show and probably many more in the years to come. You have never seen such a bull and may never again see another in your lifetime. He will sire many calves and many will be champions, I'm sure of that. Never have I seen a bull so *arrapato*, so horny! I have seen him mount three cows at one time. One after the other and all three conceived! He means more to my *patrone* than even his own wife and children. That, signore, is why the guard."

He stood up, waving the empty bottle at Carlo and shouting, "*Locandiere*, innkeeper! More grappa!"

"*Tu sei ubriaco*! You are drunk! You need no more! The bar is closed!" Carlo hollered back at him, so the fellow sat at his table, pouting.

"*Merda*! Shit! The party is over," he complained.

"Could I see this bull of yours?" I asked him.

"But of course, signore! Prepare to be amazed! Come, follow me to the truck." He stood up, almost falling, but he managed to catch himself on the table.

As I walked with him outside he staggered and nearly fell several times. The truck was parked near mine. He took out his keys, dropping them twice before finding the right one and finally unlocking the rear gate. As the door swung open, I gazed upon The Great Donetto. Never have I seen such an animal! He was every bit of what the drunken man had described him to be, a full head taller than I, and his girth was enormous! His sides nearly touched the walls of the truck. I was indeed amazed. Of course I knew he would win the prize in Arezzo. There could be none other that would even come close to this remarkable animal.

It was then an idea struck me. Was it wrong? Yes, most certainly. Would I be taking advantage of a drunken fool? Yes, absolutely. But I could not get it out of my head.

"He is indeed truly magnificent," I said, "but I do not believe that he could mount three cows at once." I turned and started to return to the inn.

"What? Do you call me a liar?" The drunken man was indignant.

"Mi scusi signore. I'm sorry, I do not mean to doubt your word, but it is quite a boast. Never in all of my years have I seen a bull do this."

"It is no boast, just the truth!" the stranger said angrily.

"It is something that I must see with my own eyes," I answered. "I will make you a bet. I have two cows in my truck. I will lead them into the pasture behind the inn. You bring your bull and if he mounts them both I will buy you a bottle of grappa. Is it a wager?"

"Done!" the stranger said. "You will see!" He slapped me on the back, smiling as he proceeded to lead Donetto out of the truck and down the ramp. We led our animals into a small fenced area behind the inn and waited.

The stranger was true to his word. Donetto caught the scent of my cows in heat immediately and mounted the first one. No sooner had the bull finished with that cow he became interested in the other. When Donetto was spent the man said, "You see?" and he laughed. "I guarantee if you had a third cow he would have his way with her as well!"

This time I did not doubt him.

"You win, signore. Let us get your bottle of grappa."

We returned our animals to our trucks and went back inside. I bought a bottle from Carlo and brought it to his table. The guard was still passed out. The man poured us a drink, and we lifted our glasses, toasting, "*Ecco il Donetto Grande*! Here's to The Great Donetto!"

The next day I arose before dawn. I barely slept anyway because I was so excited. Needless to say, I did not go to the show in Arezzo that morning. I already had what I was going for. The seed of the greatest bull in all of Italy was already at work! Besides, I did not want to take the chance of running into the man and his guard. I took my two cows home and waited. Both of the cows conceived and gave birth to males. The progeny proved to be almost as great as the father himself! That was the new beginning of the Conti Ranch stock. Unfortunately, I could not lay claim to the bloodline so I had to falsify the herd book. I have been living a lie ever since.

Teresa stared at Pietro in disbelief. She knew of the Great Donetto of course; every Italian rancher did. He is known to this day as the perfect Chianina specimen. His record size had never been equaled. Every champion bull that came after was compared to him. The fact that the entire Conti stock was based on his bloodline astonished Teresa. That Pietro had virtually stolen the bloodline of The Great Donetto amazed her even more.

"Now you see why I never entered our stock in any shows or competitions," Pietro continued. "I could not in good conscience compete under such deception and with such an unfair advantage."

Teresa finally understood. So many times Enzo and others had tried to persuade him to compete for prizes and recognition, not knowing the real reason for his stubborn refusal.

Then it came to her. Teresa knew what she needed to do and was filled with excitement at the very thought. She was sure Pietro was overcome with the same excitement when he had his similar idea so many years ago. This was the answer to Carl's and her dream. She would somehow bring the seed of the greatest Chianina of all time back to Texas!

She phoned Carl as soon as she had a moment alone. Even though it was past midnight in Texas she could not wait. Carl scarcely believed what he was hearing as Teresa retold Pietro's story. Then she explained her intention. Carl was silent for a minute then spoke.

"Teresa but how? How would it be possible? You would not only have to collect the semen without anyone's knowledge but also freeze it safely and transport it here without it thawing and spoiling. It would have to stay frozen nearly twenty four hours maybe longer if there is a delay!"

"I do not know yet Carl, but I will figure it out. Can you imagine what this could mean? Everything we have been hoping and dreaming of for so long could finally come to pass. But no one must know. No one." The two talked awhile longer and she finally hung up the phone, as it was late for Carl.

Over the next two weeks she obsessed over the idea, playing it out over and over in her mind until at last she had a plan. Would it work? She could not say for certain but if she did not at least try she could never forgive herself. Still, many details needed to be worked out and everything had to fall into place perfectly.

The following afternoon Teresa had an appointment with Pietro's lawyer in Siena. She had plenty of time, so she decided to walk around the city for a while. As she strolled through the Piazza di Campo, young people were lying on the warm stones or in groups talking and smoking. It was quiet now with only the tratorrias and outdoor cafés along the edge of the piazza attracting very many people. The next Palio was weeks away but then there would be thousands of people in this plaza to witness the greatest horse race in Italy. She made her way through to the Piazza del Duomo and, standing in front of the great gothic Cathedral de Santa Maria Assunta, she admired its beauty for the first time in many years.

Teresa loved playing tourist in her own home town, but time was passing too quickly and she needed to hurry if she was to be on time. Still, she was not worried because she knew this city so well. With a few short cuts through the streets and alley ways she could save time. But as she bustled through the narrow streets Teresa heard footsteps behind her echoing off the ancient stone walls. The steps matched her pace, so Teresa's instincts and imagination were heightened.

"Should I turn and see if the person looks dangerous or not?" she thought. No. She quickened pace and resisted the urge to turn and see her pursuer. Once again her follower matched her step for step, even as she broke into an all out run. But the streets of Siena are steep and her progress was slowed. Finally she could resist no longer and turned around just in time to see the flash of a man in dark clothing rush down another alley way and disappear.

"*E stupida donna*! You stupid woman!" she said to herself. She had frightened herself for no reason. It was just someone in as much a hurry as she was. She slowed to a normal pace, breathing heavily.

Just as she reached a blind corner a strong hand appeared, grabbed her clothing and pulled her to the sunless side of the alley. The man forced her hard against the wall with one arm under her chin and the other hand covering her mouth. He pushed his body weight against her, pinning Teresa to the hard cold stone. Her eyes were wide as she faced her attacker so closely she could smell the recent meal on his breath.

"*Buongiorno Signora Conti,*" the man said softly. He was wearing glasses so dark she could not see his eyes, even this close. He had a thick black moustache and his dark hair was slicked back under his fedora.

"It is so kind of you to return home after so many years to see to your sick uncle," he said, mocking her. "Unfortunately for some, Signore Conti's improved health has come to be a great disappointment. There are those that had hoped that nature would take its course and he would soon pass on, as old men so often do. You seem to have delayed that expectation and some grow impatient. I have been sent to bring you a message. They would hate for you to overstay your welcome in Siena and suggest that you say "*Arrivederci*" to your beloved *zio* and go back to America. This is no longer your home and you are interfering with the natural order of things. It would be wise for you to heed this advice, signora." At this the man took a step back, releasing his weight and dropping his hands. Standing silently for a few seconds looking at her, he tipped the brim of his hat, turned and slowly walked away. She stood frozen against the wall and did not move until she could no longer hear his footsteps on the old cobblestone street.

She came straight to Enzo after she had recovered from her encounter with the man on the street.

"*Bastardi!*" he shouted. "This is what I feared most Teresa. These men have no *onore*, no honor. They will stop at nothing to get what they want and what they want is the Conti Ranch and claim to the bloodline of the stock. Even the *polizia,* police will do nothing because they are being paid by them. I even suspect some of our own *butteros* could be on their payroll as well."

"They frighten me, Enzo; I will not lie to you. But if they think a strong arm man can keep me from taking my place in the Conti Famiglia they are wrong. This ranch belongs to Pietro now but the Conti family and this ranch will endure after him. This is the message we need to send, and the only way to send this message is to make this ranch stronger than ever."

"How do you plan to turn the ranch around in time Teresa? Where will you get the money we need to keep it going?" Enzo asked.

"I cannot do it without your help Vincenzo. After I am gone you must be the one who will stand up to them. The man on the street was right. I am seen as a foreigner, a temporary presence. Like a season in the year they can wait me out and I will pass. You on the other hand have a right to this land and no one will dispute that."

"I will be strong for you Teresa and for Pietro. I promise. I can manage the ranch after you have gone back to America and it will still be here when you return. Just do not be gone another twenty years." They both laughed at this and held each other for a long time.

It was time for Teresa to act on her plan. She had arranged a flight home and had let Carl know when to pick her up in Houston. The rest depended on opportunity, timing and *un sacco de fortuna*, a lot of luck. If she was successful the new Chianina crossbreeds could bring a lot of needed capital, not only for the Swanson Ranch but for the Conti Famaglia Ranch as well. It was time to pool the resources of both ranches in order to make them both strong and successful.

She went into the city to gather the necessary supplies. Having called the suppliers ahead, she knew exactly where to get what she wanted. If everything went according to plan in two days' time Teresa would be back in Texas with her prize.

Enzo was busy with the cattle. The best bulls were being selected for semen collection today. Great caution needed to be taken during this procedure. Chianina bulls can weigh nearly 1600 kg (3500 lb) and can be very dangerous. Serious accidents during this process had left many men seriously hurt and some had even been killed. The bulls can become agitated, thrashing about, kicking, or falling, and if someone gets in the way, the results can be tragic.

To gather the genetic seed for the precious bloodline, the handlers lead a teaser cow in heat into a narrow stall and tie it there. The bull is led in behind her by a rope attached to the ring through his nose. This is the most dangerous and most unpredictable moment. As the bull catches the scent of the cow in heat he can think of nothing else. He becomes single minded in his purpose and nothing will get in his way. As the bull mounts the cow the handler slips a false vagina over the bull's penis. The bull ejaculates into the false vagina, from which the semen is collected, recorded and stored until needed to artificially inseminate a selected cow.

The collection would go on most of the work day. Tonight Teresa would have to slip into the small laboratory in the barn unseen, take the semen and return to her room to prepare the precious cargo for the long journey home.

It was late and the flight out of Rome left early so the time was now. She crept from her room as quietly as possible, slinking through the house and out the back kitchen door. Until this moment, she had not been afraid, but now that the plan was in action she doubted herself just for a moment as she recognized the consequences of being caught. Pietro would be broken hearted and angry. He would once again ban her from home, this time forever. Vincenzo would feel betrayed and foolish for maintaining the trust and love he had kept for her all these years. Many would be hurt and few if any would understand.

Then there were the many unknown laws she would be breaking. She would be forced to leave Italy in disgrace and most likely would never be allowed to return. Worse, she could wind up in an Italian jail for who knows how long. Still worse, the locals who had threatened her in the alley might come seeking revenge. Who was she fooling? Teresa was no thief but here she was playing the part of one. If she was going to turn back now would be the time, but then she thought of Carl, Tony, the ranch, and their dreams. All the things she held dear gave Teresa the strength to overcome her fear and self doubt. She stepped off the back porch and headed for the barn.

Keeping to the shadows, Teresa crossed the garden and slipped into the barn. The lab was in the back, past the calving stalls. She waited until the door was closed behind her and opened the refrigerator door, bathing the small room in its weak light. There, in small vials labeled and arranged in rows, was the seed of the Conti stock and the Great Donetto. With this she would fulfill the dream Carl and she had shared for almost twenty years.

She left the lab and hurried back through the barn and out the door. Again staying in the shadows she returned to her room and put her American college education into practice. The semen needed to be protected from the freezing process so glycerol was added as an extender and Teresa now had two vials. After sealing the vials and wrapping them in black electrical tape, she uncovered a small box containing the dry ice she'd purchased earlier that day. Wearing oven mitts and using an ice pick from the kitchen, she broke off small pieces and with salad tongs packed the shards of ice into a steel coffee Thermos. Now came the alcohol which she poured slowly over the dry ice. She lowered the vials carefully into the mixture, covered them with as much of it as the container would hold and screwed on the lid as tight as she could.

It was done. If the semen survived the freezing, and if she got it through customs, and if it stayed frozen through the trip, and if the thawing process did not destroy it, and if the cow conceived after insemination, the great Donetto would produce the first of his offspring in the United States — an American Chianina. That was a lot of ifs. Was it worth the risk? She wasn't sure, but she was committed to try.

She packed the Thermos in her large suitcase with the rest of her things, and after cleaning up her little science project, got into bed and tried to sleep. It was a useless attempt. She was too excited and frightened to sleep and knew it. She lay there all night thinking and praying.

Finally, the morning came and she readied herself for the long trip home. She brought her suitcase down to the car and said goodbye to Marta. She found Pietro on the terrace, wrapped in a blanket watching the sunrise over the valley. This was his small bit of Toscana that he cherished so much. She sat with him in silence holding his hand and they took in the view as the sun crested the hills. Suddenly the valley was washed in the golden morning sunlight. The green of the vineyards lay in a patchwork of tilled tan colored earth and golden fields of hay. Cypress trees stood guard in military precision over the fields, casting their long shadows and blocking the wind. Row upon row of olive trees marched over each hill. The sunflowers were beginning to lose their bright yellow pedals and lower their faces so soon would be harvested. No matter what happened this was home. Texas may have been where her new family made its home but her heart would always live in Toscana.

She kissed Pietro on the cheek and promised to return soon. Tears fell on their faces but there was little sadness in them. They were comforted in the knowledge that Teresa would be back and that she would bring Carl and Tony so they may finally see after so many years of listening to her stories why she loved this place so and why it always would be home to her.

"*Addio Zio Pietro. Ti amo.* Goodbye Uncle Pietro. I love you," she said and hurried to the car.

117

After dropping off the rental car she checked her luggage and said a little prayer as it disappeared on the conveyor, lost among the sea of other bags. Before she knew it, she was on the plane. Soon she would be in Houston where Carl would be waiting.

As the plane took off she looked out the small window, watching as her beloved Italy passed below. Suddenly overcome with exhaustion, she slept for hours and when she awoke she did not feel refreshed but yet was excited about what was to come. "It will be quite a day ahead," she thought.

After she landed in Houston she claimed her bag and proceeded through customs. As the customs agent rifled through her suitcase he came upon the Thermos.

"What's this?' the agent asked.

In her most demure Italian accent, she answered, "I could not bear to leave home without a little Italian coffee but alas it is now cold. Is there somewhere I can pour it out?"

"Not here Ma'am. Please move on," the bored agent said. Teresa latched her bag and hurried to the exit, searching anxiously for Carl. As she passed through the doors she saw him waiting and ran into his arms. She kissed her husband long and hard.

"We must leave *now,*" she said firmly in his ear. "We must hurry."

On the drive to Calvert, she told Carl all that had happened. It became clear to Carl that he had underestimated power of the Societa della Valdichiania. He was grateful to have his wife home safe and sound after hearing about her dangerous encounter with the man on the street.

"Rodrigo is waiting for us." Carl said. "The cows in estrus have been chosen. They are midway through standing heat so now is the best time. Everything else you asked for is ready."

As they pulled into the drive to the ranch they passed the entry to the house and went directly to the barn where a make shift lab had been set up. Carl brought the suitcase to a table, opened it and brought out the Thermos. Teresa carried it to a large bowl of ice water, and as she opened the Thermos, she looked up at Carl and smiled, almost giggling.

"Still frozen," she said, relieved. "But it has begun to thaw and we cannot risk refreezing. It must be done now." With a pair of gloves she removed the two vials wrapped in black tape and placed them in the ice water. "It must thaw slowly. It will be at least two hours until it has reached the right temperature. I am exhausted and must rest. Wake me in two hours time."

She walked the short distance from the barn to the house, continued with great effort to the master bedroom, fell onto the large bed, and slipped into a deep sleep….

"Teresa! Teresa!" She heard Pietro calling but did not want to answer. Enzo and she were playing house at the old farmhouse by the pond. It was Enzo's turn to be the cook.

"Where is my dinner Enzo?" she said out loud.

The farmhouse sat on a hill on the far side of the Conti Ranch next to the big pond. It was the original villa for the estate. The Conti family bought the adjoining property at the turn of the century and this one was abandonato, abandoned, as many other old farmhouses in Tuscany had been. All throughout her childhood she had fantasized about restoring this old place and living here. It was the only place she felt at peace since Papa died. Zio Pietro's house was so big but sometimes there seemed to be so little room for her in it.

"Teresa, wake up." Carl called gently. "Teresa, it's time." She opened her eyes and cleared her head.

"Is everything ready?"

"Yes."

"Let's get started."

Teresa sat up, pulled up her boots, and followed Carl out to the barn.

"I would love a coffee," she said to Carl still groggy.

"It won't be one of yours but I'll do my best."

As Carl headed back to the kitchen, Teresa pulled the vials from the ice water, placing them in warmer water to get them to the proper temperature. Ten minutes should do it. Rodrigo had everything else ready. They would have only two chances. Two vials and two cows. Rodrigo would inseminate both Angus cows with the Conti Chianina bloodline. She loaded the two insemination catheters and handed one to Rodrigo. With his arm covered in a full-length glove, he took the loaded catheter and carefully guided it through the cervix and deposited the semen directly in the uterus. He did the same for the next cow. Now that it was done all they could do was wait.

Carl returned with the coffee.

"Did I miss all the fun?"

"Si, caro. It is done. We will know in a few weeks. If they again go into heat then we will know we have failed; if not we will have a Conti Chianina calf right here in Texas."

The next four weeks passed painfully slow. Teresa tried to keep her mind occupied with the everyday workings of the ranch but could not resist visiting the inseminated cows in the barn every day. She would just stand there and watch them in their stalls and sometimes pray.

Finally the signs of estrus could be seen in one of the cows; it was obvious she was coming into heat. Failure. The cow was not pregnant. The second cow was now their only hope. More weeks passed and the cow still had not gone into heat. At last Teresa could see that the cow was showing a larger and rounder appearance. They all agreed that the cow was indeed pregnant with a Chianina calf. Carl and Teresa held each other.

"Congratulazioni per il mio amore. Congratulations my love. We did it," she said.

"No Teresa, you did it." Carl said.

Then he kissed her deeply.

Chapter 20

After dinner Randy was walking back to the bunkhouse when he spotted Carl sitting on the veranda in the dark. He could see the occasional glow of a cigarette as Carl took a drag from it, lighting up his face with an orange glow. He walked over and sat on the floor near Carl.

"That was some story you and Teresa told us at dinner sir."

"It would not have been a very happy ending had you not come here and saved the day for us Randy. All of Teresa's effort would have been for nothing if that calf could not have been born."

"Thank you, sir."

"Call me Carl, would you Randy? This sir business reminds me too much of my old life back in Houston."

"Yes, S.." Randy stopped himself and just said "Carl."

"That's better. Besides, Randy, you've definitely earned you place here."

"Thanks, Carl. I'm not sure what I would have done if your family had not taken me in. Hank and I never talked about what to do if ever something should happen to him."

"Few of us plan for that day Randy. It's something most of us would rather not think about. Luckily I have Teresa to always see the big picture. She is the planner in the family. Funny when you think about it, your circumstances and hers are really not that much different. Both born and raised on a cattle ranch, both fathers passed away at a young age and you both went to live with another ranching family. Guess that's what makes her so strong and independent. Maybe it will do the same for you. You have much in common. Much like a son to his mother might."

"She sure knows how to take the reins that's for sure."

Randy looked up and could see Carl smile.

"That she does Randy. I will never forget when we first met. I was finishing up my last year at Texas A&M. My dorm mate invited me to a barbeque on a ranch not far from here. The Farley place, you know it?" Randy nodded and he went on. "I was a business major and almost everyone there was an Ag major so I didn't really know anyone, so I mostly just walked around and ate barbeque. The food was great and the barbeque sauce was the best I'd ever tasted. There were ribs, chicken, brisket, sausages and I tried it all.

"As I wandered away from the party, I noticed this beautiful dark haired girl up on the fence overlooking the pasture. She was standing high up, balanced on the second string of the fence gazing out over the cattle, her hair and dress blowing in the warm breeze. I wandered over and called up to her….

"How's the view from up there?" I yelled. She turned her head, looked down at me and just laughed.

"What's so funny?"

"Do you like za food?" she asked and laughed again.

"As a matter of fact I do."

"Yes I can see zat you do" she said and laughed once more. "Perhaps you should find a mirror."

"Why? Is my hair messy?" I reached up and rubbed my hair. She laughed so hard she almost fell off the fence.

"Please stop!" she said as she climbed down. "Look at your hands!" I looked down at my hands and they were covered with barbeque sauce.

"Come," she ordered, taking my arm and guiding me to where the cars were parked. She was still laughing when she pointed to the window of a car. "Do you not see yourself?" I looked in the reflection in the glass and there I was. My face was covered with barbeque sauce! Sauce was in my hair, down my chin and dripping onto my shirt.

"Perhaps you should try the salad instead." She giggled like a school girl.

I was horrified. "Have I really been walking around like this?" I cried in shame. No wonder she was laughing. I looked like a clown! She could see my embarrassment and said, "Please do not worry. We will fix it." She ran to one of the tables, grabbed some cloth napkins and took me out near the barn until she found a garden hose. As I ran my hands under the cool water she soaked the napkins and began wiping my face and hair. But all I could do was stare into her dark brown eyes while she wiped. She was even more beautiful than when I first saw her.

When she was finished she stepped back and admired her work.

"*Molto buono! Bella e pulita!* Very good! Nice and clean!"

"I'm Carl Swanson," I said. "And you are?"

"Teresa Conti." As I held out my hand she started to extend hers but then pulled it back quickly and dramatically.

"You will not eat it, will you Carl?" she said, smiling.

"That depends on the sauce it comes with."

Now both of us were laughing.

"We walked around the ranch the rest of the afternoon. She talked about her own ranch in Italy and I listened as she described Tuscany in that musical accent. She was so passionate about the land and the life there. She told me about her father and mother and her uncle Pietro. How the Conti Family had been stewards of the land for hundreds of years and how someday she would have a home of her own on that land. I fell in love with her more with every word she spoke. By the end of the day I was hopelessly in her spell.

"That day my life changed forever. Her passion gave me the strength to see what I really wanted and not just to live up to the expectations of my father. We would not have this ranch if not for her devotion to family and the patience to wait for our dream to become reality. She never let me give up on it, even in the darkest of days when I thought we would never have our own place. She made me hold on just a while longer. She sacrificed so much of herself to be with me, her home and her family. It is a debt that I can never repay."

Randy looked up at Carl and said, "I'm beginning to run up quite a tab myself."

"She really cares about you Randy. I hope you see that."

"Yeah I do and I am grateful. I felt it the first night I came here. I just hope that someday I will be able to return the favor. G'night Carl." Randy stood and walked over to the bunkhouse.

It was still dark when Randy was in the barn the next morning seeing to the new calves. Tony wouldn't be up for another hour and Teresa would be making coffee soon. He was feeling guilty about how well he had adapted to life without Hank. It was only because of what Hank taught him that he could survive now without his father's guidance. Only now had he begun to realize what a gifted teacher Hank really was. Randy had learned to be a man in a hostile world without even knowing how much Hank's lessons would help him later on. Hank believed that if you were honorable and just you would always make the right choices. So far he was right. Keeping to those boundaries made decisions remarkably easy. The choices were finite and simple.

It was time to go to the kitchen for a cappuccino with Teresa. He clung to this small ritual because it made him feel as though he belonged. It made him feel like family.

"You are early this morning Randy. The coffee is not yet ready." Teresa was just now putting on the pot.

"I will start the milk then." Randy prepared the steamed milk, and as soon as the pot stopped its airy sounds he readied the cups. "How did I ever live without these?"

"Sometimes you don't know what you are missing until someone shows you." Teresa said this as though she were talking about something else, something more personal.

"Randy, I want you to come to Italy with us. We are planning a trip in a few months after graduation and I want you to come. Please say yes."

Randy turned to her and said, "You've shown me so much in the past few months, Teresa. All I have known my whole life is within a few miles of this place. I'd like to see where you learned so much. I would also like to try one of those steaks Carl was talking about!"

"Then it is settled. We will go as a family! You are family to us Randy. I hope you know this. You have grown so much since you have come here." She reached up to his face with a dish towel. "But you still have not learned how to drink coffee without getting milk on your nose."

Later, Randy was on his way to Carl's office when he heard shouting coming from behind the office door. It was Tony and Carl. Randy felt like he was eavesdropping but could not help himself, so he stayed and listened.

"No Dad, I am not going to take the Ag courses at A&M next year! I want to apply to Rice University in Houston instead. This is not the life I want. This is *your* dream not mine! You and Mom pulled me out of my school in Houston to live out here in the sticks to raise cattle. I had no say in that decision, but I damn well have a say in this one! Don't you see that you are trying to force me the same way Grandfather forced you? "

"What do you want to do Tony, go back to Houston and follow in your Grandfather's footsteps?"

"Grandfather may have been a son-of-a-bitch, Dad, but at least he made his own way and I respect that. I know that part of your dream is a father-and-son cattle ranch, but that's not going to happen with me. I am *no* rancher and I never will be."

"How do you know unless you try Tony? Don't forget, I lived in the world that you want so badly for twenty years. It is cold and brutal and in the end you have nothing! I'm trying to build something here Tony, something that will last. How do you think it makes me feel that after I'm gone you would sell it and do God knows what with what your mother and I have worked so hard for? "

"If that's what you are afraid of, Dad, then don't leave me the ranch! Maybe you should leave it to Randy! He is more like the son you want anyway!

Suddenly the door flew open and Randy stood face to face with Tony. They just looked at each other for a moment and Tony stormed off. From the open door Randy could see Carl at his desk. His eyes were wet, disappointment and sadness showing clearly on his face. Without a word Randy reached for the door handle and gently closed the door and left Carl to his thoughts. Hank often said, "Sometimes the best thing to say to a man is nothing at all."

He gave Tony a while to cool off and then found him sitting in his car. Randy opened the passenger side door of the Caddy and slid in.

"You okay, Tony?"

"Sorry about what I said back there, Randy. I didn't mean it. You have no idea how lucky you are," he said without looking up. "Your dad loved and respected you and you knew it. Mine sees me as a stranger or worse an employee."

"That's not true, Tony. Your dad loves you. I know it. My dad was a simple man living a simple life. Things make sense when your world is as small as his was. He taught me the basics of living that I'll always be grateful for. But your dad's world is a lot bigger and a lot more complicated. He has everything riding on the success of this place and was hoping you would help him make it happen. He can't do it alone, anymore than Hank could run even our small ranch alone. They need us as much as we need them. That's the way it's supposed to be. If you can't count on each other, then you're all alone. That's how your dad feels right now."

"What do I do then, Randy? Live my life just for him?"

"Why does it have to be one or the other? Look, Tony. You're a smart guy, a lot smarter than me. There has to be a way for you to help your dad out and still live your own life. Why not look for it? Maybe you can go to Rice or A&M and learn the business end. Help your dad for a while then make your own way. You owe him that much, right? Otherwise I will get the ranch and really fuck it up. Help me out here, Brother."

Tony laughed and punched Randy hard. Randy pretended to be hurt and laughed with him.

Later that month Randy sat outside in a steel folding chair on the Calvert High football field along with one hundred and twenty of his fellow seniors. It was hot and his black cap and gown did not make it any cooler. They were sitting in alphabetical order, so Tony was seated towards the back. They began calling the names of the graduates and one by one they climbed the stairs to the stage. The principal called out, "Randall Bartlett!" and Randy walked up. As he heard his name he also heard Tony from the back whistling and screaming, "Yeah, Randy! Wooo! Hooo!"

He could also hear cheering from the audience, and when he looked up into the stadium he could see Teresa and Carl applauding and yelling. It was glorious. Hank would have been proud and with thoughts of his father Randy received his diploma.

Chapter 21

Randy came in from the pasture and went to find Teresa and Carl in the office.

"I saw the young Chianina bull out in the pasture today. He is getting bigger fast. I'd say he was up to nearly seven hundred pounds. He's getting gray around the front and his horns are coming in black. I've never seen a bull with so much muscle! I also saw him try to mount a cow, so he'll be reaching breeding age soon," he said.

"We must keep him from the cows for now, Teresa replied."Chianinas can reach puberty as early as eight months and he is past that now."

"Some of the men have been asking questions about him," Randy answered. "You're going to have to make some kind of announcement soon. I think we'd better bring him into the barn for now and keep him there until you decide what to do."

"Thanks Randy," Carl said "Give us a minute to talk about it."

"Sure."

Randy turned and left the office.

"I can't keep it from him any longer, Carl," Teresa said. "He has a right to know what I did and why I did it."

"Teresa, if you tell Pietro what we have done, you know what his reaction will be. He'll be very angry. He sees through the eyes of a traditional Italian cattle rancher; you know that those traditions have been followed for over a hundred years and he will not understand. You could lose him forever."

"Then I must at least tell Vincenzo. He might understand that we did this to help the Conti Ranch as well as our own. The money we get from these crossbreeds will strengthen the Conti Ranch so that it can never be threatened again."

"Alright, if that's what you have to do, then call him and explain. Hopefully he'll understand and support you in this."

Teresa decided to call Enzo late that night. It would be early morning in Siena and he would be home.

Chapter 22

At the Conti Ranch in the early hours, Sofia and her husband were discussing their daughter's latest suitor.

"Sofia, must he be here so early? Enzo asked.

"Enzo, you must face the fact that you have been cursed with a beautiful daughter. She cannot help it if boys want to be around her all the time. Besides Stefano is a handsome boy and comes from a good family. We could do much worse."

"I am not so certain. After all, his father is Roberto Graso, head of one of the families that wants to expand their land holdings to include the Conti Ranch. He has made that desire very clear."

"Marcella!" Sofia called. "Stefano is coming up the walk."

"Yes Mama I saw him coming from my window. He is giving me a ride to school this morning," she called back.

"Tell him to wait outside. Your father has not yet finished his breakfast."

Marcella instructed Stefano to wait at the kitchen door and she would be out.

The phone rang and Enzo answered it.

"Teresa! It's good to hear your voice. They are all well grazie. Of course I am listening. Tell me what's on your mind." There was a long silence as Enzo listened carefully to what Teresa was telling him. His eyes widened and his heart raced as she told him what she had done. He did not interrupt as she explained and when she was finally finished he spoke.

"Teresa, how could you do this? Do you truly know what this means? This is a serious violation of all our breeding practices and traditions! Not to mention the laws you may have broken! We noticed that a semen sample that was recorded was missing but simply thought it an error and let it pass. Now you tell me you stole it and took it to America and that you have a Chianina crossbreed at your ranch in Texas? I do not know what to say to you. Yes, I know we need money for the ranch but there must have been some other way. Of course Pietro must not know. It would kill him to hear what you have done. I cannot discuss this now, I must think a while. I will call back later."

Enzo hung up the phone and stood in the small kitchen, unable to move. He was desperately trying to make sense of what he had been told. He also did not notice that the kitchen door was slightly ajar and Stefano Graso was standing right behind it.

A week had gone by since Teresa had spoken to Enzo. He made his feelings clear that he was disappointed in what she had done. He felt that she did not trust him enough to at least discuss it with him first. He was hurt and angry and insisted that this be the end of it. The half breed must be the last of his kind, and he could not be swayed on this. She was hoping he could be persuaded enough to see her point of view, to see the possibilities and advantages of what they were trying to accomplish. But even after his anger had subsided his opinion did not change. She was at a loss for what to do next. She and Carl must decide whether to go forward with the plan to breed the bull or not. If they did, it would be without Enzo's consent. If they did not, everything they had done to this point would have been for nothing.

Teresa, Carl and Randy were in the barn at the bull's stall.

"He sure is somethin'." Randy said. "Just look at the muscle! He's grown so fast! You say in another year he'll be twice this size?"

"Yes, he is magnificent. Much as the bulls in Siena but different too, more compact. His head is squarer than the purebreds and he is not as tall. He has much of what makes the Chianina special but in a more manageable size." Teresa said. "I will call him Dante after the great Italian poet."

"What do we do Teresa?" Carl asked. "Is this going to be the last crossbreed? Should we castrate him or simply put him down and invite the neighbors for a big barbeque?" He was obviously frustrated. Here was the goal, the prize, and they were discussing giving it up. It pissed him off.

"We do not have to decide today Carl." Teresa said firmly. "As long as Dante is separated from the herd we can consider all of our options."

Chapter 23

Randy was asleep in the bunkhouse when he was awakened by noise coming from the barn. Cows were mooing and the horses were restless. He looked out of his small window in the direction of the barn and saw lights and movement. Someone with a flash light was in the barn. Quickly he dressed, pulled on his boots and went out to see what was happening. When he reached the side door to the barn he heard another door open in the back and knew something was wrong. As he ran back out and around to the rear of the barn and saw a dark figure disappearing out of the range of the outside barn light.

Randy hurriedly returned to the barn and reached for the light panel on the wall. He threw all the switches at once and the entire barn was instantly lit up. The first thing he saw when the lights came on was the bloody footprints on the floor leading out the back door. Randy ran though the barn, tracing the footprints back to their source.

He stopped when they ended at the stall of the young Chianina bull. The floor was covered in blood. The pool was still spreading out of the stall and out to the main walkway. On the floor of the stall lay Dante. His throat had been slit and blood was still draining from the gaping wound onto the floor. Dante's glassy eyes were open and his flaccid pink tongue hung loose from his open mouth.

The sight of the dead bull froze Randy for a second as his mind tried to deny what his eyes were telling him. He turned and ran toward the back where he saw the dark figure escape into the night. Someone was running through the pasture in the direction of the main road to the ranch.

Randy heard voices coming from the front of the barn and ran to meet them. Hastily dressed, Carl and Teresa hurried toward him. Carl was carrying a shotgun.

"Randy! What's happening?" Carl shouted.

"Someone killed Dante and ran out into the pasture! They must have a car parked on the road!" Randy yelled back.

Tony, wearing pants but no shirt, appeared in the driveway and rushed to the scene. Turning, Carl ran to his truck with his shotgun. He saw Tony's car blocking the drive.

"Tony! Move your car now!"

"Just take it!" Tony yelled back and tossed Carl the keys.

"Carl, no!" Teresa shouted. "Don't follow him. Let him go. He may be dangerous! Randy! Stop him!"

Randy ran in Carl's direction but was too late. Carl had already started the car as Tony jumped in the passenger side. Gravel flew, and the Caddy tore down the drive at breakneck speed, throwing rocks high into the air. The tires screamed as they found pavement and the car rocketed down the road, high beams piercing the darkness with bright red taillights bringing up the rear. Randy could hear the powerful engine roar as Carl floored the accelerator.

Teresa rushed into the barn with Randy close behind. She stopped at the stall and fell to her knees as she saw the spreading pool of blood surrounding Dante. As the blood reached her she did not get up. Instead she dropped her head, brought her hands to her face and wept.

Randy was at a loss for what to do for her. Consoling a grief stricken woman was something he'd never done in his young life. It was a lesson Hank hadn't gotten to yet. He knelt down, wrapped his arms around her and lifted her from the floor. Her knees were soaked in the blood of her great prize. He guided her out of the barn and into the house.

"We need to call the State Troopers," Randy said, and he reached for the phone on the kitchen wall.

"Yes. That's right," he was saying into the phone. "They took off after the guy and are in a white Cadillac, heading south on the Texas Six. Please stop them before somebody gets hurt!"

Teresa was only hearing bits and pieces of what Randy was saying into the phone as her mind was reeling with the events of this awful night....

Chapter 24

Carl caught the keys Tony had tossed him. He heard Teresa shouting to him but did not stop. Dropping the shotgun on the seat, he jumped behind the wheel of the Caddy and started the engine just as a shirtless Tony slid into the seat next to him.

"No, Tony. Stay here with your mother." Carl said sharply.

"It's my ranch, too. Right, Dad? Besides, Randy's here. He'll look after Mom."

Carl looked into Tony's eyes, nodded, threw the lever into drive and sped down the driveway much faster than he knew he should have. The gravel hitting the undercarriage sounded like machine gun fire. Once on the pavement he floored the accelerator and the tires screamed in protest.

Dante's murderer had to cross the pasture on foot before reaching his car at the road. Even at a full run it would have taken two or even three minutes. That meant he was less than a minute ahead of them. At 4:00 o'clock in the morning there would be no other cars out, only his and the Caddy. Carl quickly reached eighty miles per hour and kept accelerating, ninety, one hundred. Suddenly up ahead were tail lights. The driver was doing at least eighty. There was no other reason to be going that fast unless you were trying to get away from something or someone.

"There he is!" Tony shouted.

"I see that son of a bitch," Carl said, gripping the wheel tighter.

The powerful Caddy was catching up fast, two hundred yards and closing.

At that moment the high beams lit up a green and yellow John Deere tractor getting ready to cross the highway in front of the Caddy.

"Look out!" Tony screamed.

Carl turned the wheel and missed the tractor by inches but the turn was too sharp and he was going way too fast. The Caddy went into a sideways skid, caught traction and flipped over once, twice, three times. The widows blew out as the hood was crushed. The passenger door flew open and the centrifugal force ejected Tony from the car. He felt a sense of weightlessness and then a bone shattering landing. Tony fell to rest twenty feet from the smoking wreckage that was his car. He was lying on his back and could see the stars above him. He turned his head to look in the direction of the car and could see Carl hanging half out of the door upside down, eyes wide, staring at nothing. Tony knew his father was dead. He felt no pain, only a sudden sleepiness, and he couldn't resist closing his eyes.

Chapter 25

Randy found himself in the same hospital he was in a little more than a year ago with Tony. This time Tony was not sitting with him in the waiting room; he was in the operating room. It had been hours since the ambulance brought him here and the emergency surgery began. Carl was gone. Randy couldn't believe it. So much had happened in so short a time. No time to even process it all.

Teresa, overcome with grief, had collapsed when the state troopers came to the ranch with news of the crash. To see someone as strong as Teresa so devastated as to be unreachable and inconsolable broke Randy's heart. A doctor called to the house gave Teresa a strong sedative, but when she awakened her grief would begin again in earnest. Hopefully by then Tony would be out of surgery with good news from the doctors, but in Randy's experience doctors rarely brought good news. Randy's new family had been shattered in one terrible night. It seemed he was destined to be without one.

Finally Tony was in recovery but still in a coma. Over the course of the next few days if Teresa was not at Tony's side she would lock herself in her room and not come out. Randy had never felt so helpless. He could do nothing for either of them. Soft crying sounds would come from Teresa's room and Randy would sit in a chair near the door, waiting for her to emerge from her dark grief. They would go to the hospital together and sit in Tony's room even though he did not know they were there. So much silence it was deafening.

Once again Randy found himself wearing Carl's black suit. The funeral was held in Houston, since the

Swansons had no family and few friends in Calvert. He was buried next to his father. Teresa did not talk to many people. The only real friend she had in this country was Carl. He was everything to her.

A few days after the funeral, Tony began showing signs of consciousness. Soon after that he was fully awake and talking. Teresa met with the doctors and true to form they did not have good news to offer. Tony had broken his back in several places and damaged his spinal cord. He was now paralyzed from the waist down; most likely permanently. The young man took the news badly, first by crying, then by screaming, and finally by not saying anything at all.

Randy had been helping to keep the ranch going. Earl Perkins was grateful for the help because some of the men had decided to leave after Carl died and he was short handed. The job helped him keep his mind occupied, so he worked long days. The nights were the hardest when he was left alone with his thoughts.

Earl told him that he would be leaving soon himself in a few days. His brother had a small spread up in Montana and he was going up there to help run it.

"You're always welcome to come with me, Randy. We could sure use a man like you."

"Thanks, Earl, but Teresa will need me here."

Randy shook Earl's hand and wished him luck.

Finally, the doctors could do no more for Tony so Teresa brought him home. Randy came to his room on the day he returned home from the hospital. He knocked on the door but there was no response. After knocking again without an answer he slowly pushed the door open.

"Tony? You awake?"

"Yeah Randy I'm awake."

"I just wanted to say how glad I am to see you Tony. I've missed you."

"You have? Really?" Tony said with sarcasm.

"Yeah, I have. It hasn't been the same around here without you."

"I would have thought maybe you wished I didn't come home at all, Randy. In fact I thought maybe you wished I had died. God knows I do."

"What are you talking about, Tony?"

"Seems pretty simple, Brother. With me out the way you get pretty much everything you wanted." He started getting louder. "Now you can be the big shot rancher and run the whole place."

"That's not true." Randy answered calmly, but visibly hurt. "You're not thinking straight. How can you say something like that?"

"If it weren't for you, Randy, none of this would have happened. If you had never come here that damn bull would have died at birth, my dad would still be alive, and I wouldn't be like this!" He was screaming now. Teresa heard the noise and rushed into the room.

"What's going on in here? Tony, please, calm down. You are getting all worked up." Teresa said. "Randy, please go now. Come back later when he is not so upset."

"Yeah, Randy. Get the fuck out! Don't come back at all, ever! As a matter of fact I want you off this ranch today! I mean it. I don't ever want to see your face around here again! Get out! Get out!" Tony shouted.

Randy backed out of the room in shock, turned, and ran from the house. He could not believe that he had just heard what his best friend had said to him. Did Tony really believe that Randy wanted the ranch for himself? Did he really blame him for the accident? He could not stay here a minute longer if that were true.

Suddenly it felt as though his whole world were crashing in around him. He had to get away! He could not live with the blame for all that had happened, real or imagined.

Earl was packing up his truck and getting ready to leave. Randy trotted over to him.

"That offer still stand, Earl?"

"Shore does Randy, but I gotta hit the road soon. It's a long haul to Montana."

"Give me five minutes to get my gear and we can leave."

Randy ran to the bunkhouse quickly, packed up his things, gathered all the money he had saved, and hustled back to the truck. He threw his bag in the back and jumped into the cab.

"Adios Texas! Hola Montana!" Earl shouted as they started down the gravel driveway.

Randy had the sudden urge to stop the truck and find Teresa, to tell her how sorry he was for everything. He wanted to thank her for saving his life when Hank died and for teaching him so many things. Most of all he wanted to tell her how much he loved her and how much he would miss her. He knew he couldn't do that to her or himself. The Swanson's didn't need any more pain and neither did he. It was better this way. He would just be gone and maybe Tony would get better. Maybe they could be a family again without him around to remind them of everything that had happened these past few weeks. Without him they could move on.

When the truck hit pavement Randy looked back. For the second time in his young life he had lost his home and his family. He pulled his hat down over his eyes and pretended he was going to take a nap. He did not want Earl to see his tears.

Chapter 26

Seven years later, Randy's life in Montana had come and gone, leaving no special memories. The hard work helped mask the memories of the past but now being home has brought it all back. At the Swanson Ranch, Tony was giving Randy nothing but bad attitude and precious little information.

"Let's go for a walk, Tony."

"Sorry, Bro. No can do," he said with an extra dose of sarcasm.

"A roll then." Randy took hold of the handles on the wheelchair and brought Tony outside into the blinding Texas sunshine. Locking the wheels of Tony's chair he crossed the gravel drive.

"Remember the old football days, Tony? I always watched your back on the field and you never once got hurt. I held up my end of the deal." Randy walked twenty yards over to the truck and rifled through his duffel bag. He came up with a beat up football and tossed it up and down. Tony looked at him and frowned, not getting where Randy was going with this.

"What your point Bartlett?

"Think fast, Swanson!" Randy yelled, and he threw the football as hard as he could at Tony. Tony's eyes widened as he saw the ball being thrown in his direction. Wheels locked there was no escape. It hit him square in the chest. Either by remembered reflexes or by pure luck he caught the deadly spiral. An audible "*Oomph*!" escaped him as the air was pushed from his lungs. The force of the pass knocked the wheel chair backward with Tony on his back still in a seated position holding the ball and looking up at icy blue

Texas sky. The wind had been knocked out of him so he couldn't speak. All he could do was make little gasping sounds as his lungs desperately tried to regain function and refill with precious oxygen.

Randy slowly strolled over to Tony. The only sounds were his boots crunching on the gravel with each step and the wheezing sounds escaping from Tony's tortured lungs. Randy leaned in over his friend's head, watching him gasping for a few seconds, frowned with detached interest and said only, "Nice catch."

Just then Tony took a deep breath, regained his voice and screamed, "Are you out of your fucking mind Randy?! Are you trying to kill me for fuck's sake?!"

Randy just looked down and pointed his finger at him.

"I owed you that one, Brother! Pay back is a bitch. Ain't it?!"

Tony stared at him blankly for a few seconds. When suddenly his memory of that hot August morning on the Calvert High football field so many years ago kicked in and he broke into uncontrollable laughter. Tears streamed from his eyes as Randy joined in and laughed so hard he could not stand. He fell next to Tony, holding his splitting sides. A dark wet spot grew in Randy's lap. He had just pissed himself. Tony saw this and started another round of laughter, pointing at Randy's wet crotch. After a few moments they regained control of themselves, breathing heavily with the last few chuckles.

Randy stood and picked up the wheelchair so that Tony was again upright. He squatted down in front of him, reached out and held his face in his large hands.

"I love you, Tony, and I always will. There is nothing you can ever do or say that will change that."

Tony looked into Randy's eyes. Both men were crying now.

"You left me here, Randy," Tony said through his tears. "You left me here all alone to rot. I missed you so much and you were not here for me when I needed you most."

"I know, Brother. I'm so sorry. Never again," Randy choked. They held each other forehead to forehead like they would never let go.

Randy wheeled his friend back into the big house. Seeing Tony's exhaustion, Randy helped him to his room to rest. Then he fired up the old pizza oven, loading it with wood lighting the kindling. He made the dough and while it rose and the oven was heating, he went to the store for some supplies. When he returned he made a large salad, readied the dough and rolled out a big pizza crust. He loaded it up with all his and Tony's favorite toppings and cheese then slid it into the *forno*. With the long handled peel, *pala di legno*, wooden paddle he turned the pizza quickly so it wouldn't burn in a hot spot. After only a few minutes it was done to perfection. He got Tony up, brought the pizza inside and placed it on the table within easy reach of his brother.

"My God, Randy, Mom really taught you well!"

"She taught me a lot more than how to cook Tony. Even though I've been gone a long time I can still hear her voice every day. She's had just as much of an influence on my life as Hank did. That's why I'm here now."

After they had eaten their fill of pizza, Randy said, "Ok Tony what have I missed? Why did you call me for help?"

Tony took a deep breath and began.

"After you left things got pretty bad for a while. I was not adjusting well to my new limitations and we fought a lot about it. Mom still had to keep the ranch going so she threw herself into that and we drifted apart. Finally after about six months she came to my room and told me I was going to go back to school. I refused and we argued about it for weeks. Then in her usual Teresa Conti fashion she said the choice was no longer mine to make.

"She got me into Texas A&M and I started taking the business courses I had planned on before the accident. At first I resisted but after awhile my interest overcame my anger and I decided that I would pursue my business degree at Mays just like Dad did. I worked hard, rolled around campus alone and feeling like an outcast but got through it. It gave me a sense of purpose that nothing else in my life did. The next four years was all work for me. I took summer classes and did anything I could to stay on track to get my degree.

"About a year after the accident Mom sold the stock to Malcolm Farley. We kept a small amount of cattle to maintain our tax status as a producer. We have one full-time man and two part-timers to maintain the ranch.

"Finally I graduated from A&M with honors and spent another two years getting my Masters Degree. When I tried to find work, no one wanted to hire me no matter what my credentials were. They just could not see past the chair. After about a year I just gave up and stayed here and stopped trying.

"Mom's life was no better. The ranch was her and Dad's dream and after he died she lost her passion for it. She was just going through the motions while I finished school. About a year ago her Uncle Pietro died and she went back to Italy for his funeral. She was only gone a few weeks but when she came back she had a renewed energy about her, like she had gotten a jumpstart to life. I think it was being back home that did it. It recharged her somehow. You know how she always talked about her life there and what it meant to her. Things made sense for her in Tuscany like they never did here. I'm not so sure she ever really belonged here at all. It was only the love she had for my Dad that kept her here in Texas. That and the obligation she felt for me.

"Dad had a hefty insurance policy. It paid off the ranch and kept the Conti ranch in Italy afloat. She even paid the taxes on your ranch hoping you would come home someday. Otherwise that state would have taken it."

Randy had never even thought of that. Like always, Teresa took care of things.

He continued.

"One night she came to my room and told me she was going back to Siena permanently and asked me to come with her. I said no of course. If I couldn't get my life together here, how could I ever do it in Italy? There was a part of me that wanted to be happy for her but I was selfish and made her feel guilty for leaving.

"The next two months we worked to wind down the ranch and leased out most of the pasture land."

"Okay, that gets me up to speed on you and the ranch but what about Teresa? What kind of trouble is she in and how can I help?" Randy asked.

"You already know about the other ranchers in Tuscany and the control they have on the cattle business there. They have been after the Conti family land holdings for years, and after Pietro died they thought they could make their move but they underestimated Teresa."

"No surprise there."

"I know, right?"

"Anyway, she fought them at every turn. She even rallied the smaller ranchers to her side and formed a group of families that were willing to fight for themselves and resist the takeover.

"Now it gets ugly. The Graso Family and a few other larger landholders have decided to take the land by any means. They're playing hardball, Randy. Threats, intimidation, beatings, and even a few mysterious deaths. Then, last week when Mom was coming home from the city someone ran her off the road. It was a clear attempt to kill her and get her out of the way. She wrecked her car and has a few bumps and bruises, but she's okay. Next time she might not be so lucky. These are the same people responsible for killing the Chianina crossbreed. I know it.

"That's when I found Earl's brother in Montana and called you. I didn't know who else would be willing to help her. I'm asking you to go to Italy and protect her, Randy. You can't say no. You can't call her and tell her you're coming either or she won't let you."

Tony was right. Randy couldn't say no. The thought of traveling to a foreign country and playing bodyguard for Teresa scared the shit out of him, but there was nobody else.

When Randy was a kid, Hank once told him a story about the war. He said, "When you owe someone your life, you are obligated to protect them with yours." If the present situation didn't fit that scenario he didn't know what did.

That night Randy arranged for a one way flight to Rome. Luckily he still had his passport that Teresa had gotten him when they were planning their trip after graduation before the accident. Tony gave him all the addresses and phone numbers in Siena he needed.

Randy called Earl in Montana and told him that he wasn't coming back, so Earl made arrangements to pick up his truck from the Houston airport where Randy would leave it. Earl wished him luck and hoped he would come back soon. Randy couldn't make that promise, but he hoped to just the same.

The next day after saying his goodbyes to Tony he decided to make a stop on the way to the airport. Once again he passed the old Bartlett mailbox and drove up to the house. After retrieving the key from the coffee can he let himself in and went straight to Hank's room. Going through the dresser, he found the key to the green ammo box, pulled it down from the shelf, opened it, and removed Hank's .45. He attached the slide and pushed the empty magazine into the grip. Holding the gun in his right hand as Hank had shown him so many years ago, he pulled back the slide with his left, cocking the hammer. He pointed the gun at his reflection in the dresser mirror and pulled the trigger. *Click!* It was the only sound in the ghostly silent house.

On the way to the airport he stopped at a sporting goods store and bought two boxes of .45 caliber cartridges for the gun. He stuffed the gun into his left black dress boot and the boxes of ammo in the right. He then put the boots at the bottom of his duffel bag.

When he got to the airport he left the truck keys under the mat so a driver could pick up Earl's truck. He checked his bag at the curb and went to his gate.

Randy had never been on a plane before in his life and wished he was going under different circumstances.

Once on the plane and in the air, Randy thought about Hank. What would he say about all of this? I'm sure he would say something profound like. "Randy, a man's gotta do what a man's gotta do."

"Thanks Hank," he thought to himself, "but I think this time that old cowboy sage advice just doesn't help at all."

Chapter 27

After landing in Rome and with some difficulty Randy made his way to the train that would take him to Siena. He felt out of sorts. He was tired and sleepy, yet it was the middle of the day. With his up-at-dawn body clock, the time change wasn't going to be easy.

What Tony told him was a two hour drive by car turned out to be four by train but Randy didn't mind. He hadn't known what to expect Italy to look like except from what Teresa had told him, but the land was not so strange. As a matter of fact it seemed rather familiar once the train left the crowded city and began to give way to the farms and hills.

He and Earl had driven to Northern California once to a ranch owned by a friend of his in the Sonoma area and this land had a similar feel in many ways. The rolling rocky hills mixed with oak trees had a striking resemblance.

As the train traveled north, the hills became more dramatic, dotted with what looked like medieval castles at the highest points. Teresa had shown him pictures in books and those photographic images came back to him, giving him a point of reference, but they did not do the land or the view justice. The farther the train carried him the more beautiful the scenery became. To the east, the hills were forming into small forested mountains looking down to the farms on the lush valley floor. He looked around the train car at his fellow travelers reading their papers or napping and ignoring the scenery because they had seen it a thousand times before, taking it for granted. He was seeing it with new eyes of discovery as an infant might see something for the first time and becomes fascinated by it.

As they came into the station at Siena, Randy got off the train and was instantly lost, a stranger in a city that did not speak his only language. The conversations around him were incomprehensible. He watched as other travelers loaded onto buses from the station marked Siena Centro and assumed that was the thing to do, so he did the same. He fumbled with the foreign money that he did not understand at all, but with the help of the driver he paid his fare and got onto the bus. It was a short uphill ride to the city center and from there he did the only thing that made sense to him and found a taxi that would take him to the Conti Villa.

Randy was glued to the window of the taxi cab as they drove through the city. It was busy, yet at the same time there was an easy calm about it. Driving back down the hill to the roads leading to the outlying countryside he got a good view of the oldest section of Siena. The domed church and the ancient tower dominated this part of the city and could be seen from almost every angle. He would ask Teresa to show him around once he got settled.

Just then he remembered that she had no idea he was coming. He had not seen her in years and showing up in Italy like this would be more than a little surprising for her. The anticipation of seeing her was both exciting and frightening because he was unsure how she would react, especially once he told her that Tony had called him and why he had come. She may be more than a little angry. He had only seen her angry a few times before and he did want to be the on the receiving end of her fury.

As the city gave way to more open space Randy watched as they passed small farms and cottages. Grape vineyards were everywhere, some only a few acres surrounding a villa or house and others that went for miles cresting one hill after the other. Gnarled olive trees began to dominate the landscape and the drab green leaves contrasted with the yellow dry grass. Soon pasture land opened up and he began to see the first signs of cattle. The huge white and gray animals grazed lazily on the grass. Randy finally saw what Teresa had been describing years ago when she spoke of these majestic creatures. He could not wait to get up close to them and experience them first hand.

The taxi pulled into the gate of the villa and up to the house. "Conti," the driver said pointing toward the huge front door. Randy awkwardly paid the fare and the cab driver smiled and said "*buono fortuna*, cowboy" as he drove away.

Randy carried his duffel bag to the door and knocked using the big iron ring. An old woman came to the door and her eyes widened as she stared at him. She looked up at his Stetson then down to his boots and back up to his face.

"*Casa passo fare voi, signore?* Can I help you sir?"

"I'd like to see Mrs. Swanson please Ma'am."

"Meeses Swanson?" Marta said. *"Oh! Signora Conti! Si?"*

"Yes Ma'am."

"La Signora Conti non e a casa," Marta shook her head.

Randy knew enough Spanish and that was pretty close so he understood that Teresa was not home.

"Can you tell me where I could find Vincenzo Conti?"

"Enzo! Si, si. Lungo la strada!" She pointed down the drive and the dirt road beyond.

Randy got that he lived just down the road so he tipped his hat and started walking.

It was warm but no worse than Texas in summer so he didn't mind the heat as he strolled down the dirt road. Not far from the Conti Villa he came to a smaller stone farmhouse that looked neat and well lived in. He walked up to the door and knocked. A stout middle aged man opened the door only half way and eyed him with suspicion. He did not speak so Randy asked him.

"Vincenzo Conti?

"Si. And you are?"

Randy was relieved to hear English and smiled broadly.

"I'm Randy Bartlett sir, a friend of Teresa's."

"Randy Bartlett? The cowboy from Texas?" Enzo relaxed and met Randy's smile with his own. Randy nodded and he shook Enzo's hand.

"Yes, sir. That's me."

"Teresa has spoken of you often Randy, please come in out of the heat."

As he entered the old stone house Randy felt instantly at ease. The house had a natural comfort to it. Wooden beams, stone walls and red clay floor tiles came together in a cozy way that he liked immediately. It was darker and cooler inside than he expected and his eyes adjusted to the change. He took off his hat as a woman entered the room.

"Sofia this is Randy Bartlett, Teresa's friend from Texas."

"Buongiorno Signore Randy," Sofia said. *"Una bibita fresca?"* A cool drink? She made a drinking gesture with her hand and Randy understood.

156

"Yes ma'am that would be nice." He nodded. "Thank you."

"Prego."

Sofia brought him a glass of cool water and Randy drank half of it in one gulp.

"Teresa did not tell me you were coming, Signore Randy. Is she expecting you?"

"No sir she's not. Her son Tony called me and told me she might be in some kind of trouble here and asked me to check up on her."

"I am not sure if you can help with the kind of trouble she has here, Randy."

"What do you mean, sir?"

"There are people in Siena, Randy, that want our famiglia lands badly and by any means. They have hurt and intimidated some of our butterros and threatened their families. They have even made threats against mine. This is why I am not far from my home at any time and keep this ready." He pointed to an old double barrel shotgun leaned behind the door. Most likely he had his hands on it when Randy had knocked.

"My daughter lives in town and has been harassed by some of Roberto Graso's men, so she had to come here and stay with us. My son has been provoked into fights and has been beaten twice now, so I sent him to school in Florence. Tony must have also told you about Teresa's accident, but we all know it was no accident at all. Someone tried to run her off the road. She could have been seriously hurt or worse."

"Where is Teresa now, sir?"

"Please call me Enzo, Randy. Teresa has talked about you as though you are famiglia and I want us to be friends as well." Randy smiled and asked again.

"So where is she, Enzo?"

"She has gone to Roberto Graso's office in town to try and reason with him in hopes that he will call off his men and stop the intimidation. She demanded that I stay here and protect my family while she was gone."

"She went alone?" Randy asked. He was half surprised and half angry that she would be allowed to do this on her own without protection. But mostly he was just concerned for her safety. If these were the men behind the bull killing back in Texas and the recent attempt to run her down, there was no telling what else they would be capable of.

"I need to go to her now," Randy said firmly.

"I will not leave my family alone, but I will have my daughter drive you to his office and let you out. But she must return home as soon as she has done so. I do not want her on the street. They know her well and she will not be safe in town. She is out in the garden. I will tell her what we are doing." Enzo left the room and Sofia was nowhere in sight. Randy opened his duffel bag and retrieved Hank's .45 from his dress boot. He pulled out his tucked in shirt so that the tail was hanging over his pants and stuffed the gun in his waistband. It was not comfortable but it was hidden well enough.

He heard voices and then the kitchen door opened. Enzo came in, followed by a woman. He stood as they entered the room.

"This is Marcella, my daughter," Enzo said.

Randy was stunned. Dressed in jeans, work shirt tied at the navel and heavy boots was the most beautiful young woman he had ever seen. Her hair was thick and black with waves of curls that went past her shoulders. Her eyes were the deepest ocean blue and the contrast of hair and eyes was remarkable. Her wine colored lips were full and ripe. All he could do was nod and say, "Hello, Miss."

Enzo had seen this look before on the faces of other young men when they meet his daughter. He rolled his eyes.

"Randy. Randy! Enzo said loudly, clapping his hands to get the young man's attention. "Marcella will drive you into town and show you where the Graso offices are, but she must return immediately. Do you understand me?"

"Yes, sir," Randy said and he and Marcella went outside to the car.

As they left the drive and got onto the dirt road, Randy did not speak. He knew little Italian and would not know what to say to this woman anyway. She handled the little Fiat as though it were a race car, shifting smoothly and expertly. Dust clouds flew from the rear tires. Marcella glanced over to him as she drove and he looked into her eyes but quickly looked away. It surprised him when she spoke in perfect English.

"Zia Teresa has spoken of you often. She has said you have a great talent with the cattle. She also says that she has not seen you for a very long time. I have seen her sad over this."

"I've been away."

"Yes, she has said that. She also hoped that you would return home soon."

"Look. I'm not sure how much you know about me or what happened at the Swanson Ranch and I owe Teresa, but I don't owe any explanations, okay?"

Marcella lifted the corner of her mouth and half smiled.

"Okay, Randy. *Capisico*. I understand."

They came off the dirt and on to the main road to town.

"What do you know about these people?" he asked her.

"Only that they are dangerous and have the protection of the *polizia*. Zia Teresa has fought them for the past year but they are relentless. They want our land and as far as they are concerned they will have it. You do not have men like this in America?"

"There are men like that everywhere. They are all the same," Randy said.

"How will you stop them?"

"I am not here to stop them. I am here only to be sure Teresa is not hurt. The land is not my concern."

"But Randy, the Conti land and Zia Teresa are one in the same. You cannot protect one without protecting the other."

Marcella drove into the heart of the city, parked in a small alley way and got out of the car. Randy stopped her.

"Get back in the car Marcella, your father's orders. Go home."

"I have some news for you, Randy. I do not take orders from you, and I do not often listen to my father either." She just stood and stared at him, daring him to challenge her. "*Zia* Teresa is not only my aunt but she is also my best friend. If she is in trouble I will not abandon her, and you cannot stop me."

Randy wanted no part of trying to exert control over this woman who was hell bent on protecting Teresa. He could see the family resemblance and recognized the futility of trying to force her to go home. He would have to keep her safe somehow.

"I don't know what's going on in there but if there is any trouble I want you to stay close to Teresa and don't do anything stupid. Okay? Your father is going to shoot me with that shotgun of his if something should happen to you. *Capisco*? Understand?"

"Yes Randy. I understand." She had won easily. This young cowboy did not stand a chance.

They entered a small stairway that led up to the second floor. Through the heavy doors Randy could hear shouting in Italian. First a woman's voice; that must be Teresa. Then a man's voice; loud and threatening. He looked at Marcella and her eyes were wide and frightened. They both heard a loud slap and Teresa cried out. Randy pushed Marcella aside, took a step back, raised his foot and kicked the door at the latch. The old wood splintered easily and flew open. Three shocked faces turned toward him as he made his entrance. Inside the room an older gray haired man stood behind a large ornate desk. A younger man with a thick black mustache and slick backed hair loomed over Teresa.

"Randy!" Teresa yelled. "*In nome di Dio, ci fai qui?!* What in the name of God are you doing here?!"

"I'm just on vacation Teresa, so I thought I'd stop by and see an old friend. I hope I'm not interrupting anything."

Teresa saw Marcella standing in the hall and her eyes went back to Randy. His boots were silent as he strolled across the deep antique carpet and stood next her.

"So the cavalry has arrived from Texas just like in the American movies," the younger man said with a big smile. "Then this must be John Wayne." Both men laughed. "I once made a visit to Texas to see a sick friend. Unfortunately he died in my arms." The man laughed again.

Randy knew he was facing the man that slit Dante's throat that awful night. That brutal act had ruined the last seven years of his life and the anger he felt was rising fast. Randy moved closer to Teresa. She was holding one hand to her face and there were tears in her eyes. He brought her hand down and his could see clearly the reddened hand print on her face. He looked over at the two men and gave them a quick evaluation. Clearly the younger one was the most dangerous so that was his target.

In one quick motion he reached under his shirt, pulled the .45 from his waistband, and brought the slide back, cocking the hammer with its distinctive sound. Shoving the younger man hard up against the wall, he pressed the barrel of the gun to his forehead.

"If I'm John Wayne, then that makes me the good guy, doesn't it? So I guess that makes you the bad guy, right?" The man said nothing. His eyes were wild with fear.

"We all know what happens to the bad guys in all of the John Wayne movies, don't we? They always end up dead." Randy pushed the barrel harder into the man's head. The sound of water could be heard at his feet. Squinting in terror, the young thug grimaced as he tried to turn away from the gun.

"Don't turn away, mister. That only makes killin' you easier, and you want it to be *very* hard for me to do. Killin' a man should be the hardest thing in the world. But sometimes it just has to get done."

The terrified man opened his eyes once more and Randy pulled the gun away but kept it pointed at him. There was a bright red circle clearly imprinted on his forehead from the cold barrel. Randy could see a dark spot on the man's pants and the urine on the floor. He smiled.

Meanwhile, Marcella had rushed toward Teresa. She wrapped her arms around her and guided her to the door. When they had passed the doorway Randy backed out after them, still holding his gun high.

"If anyone comes near the Conti family again I will not hesitate to come back here and kill you both. For your sakes you should believe that."

Randy left the room and hurried downstairs to Teresa and Marcella, waiting by the car. He got into the back seat and Marcella drove them out of the city as if she were Mario Andretti himself.

Panting, Marcella said, "I have never seen anything like that in all my life!"

"That makes two of us." Randy said quietly. He was breathing heavily too and trying to calm his nerves.

"Randy have you lost your mind!?" Teresa had recovered and was now getting back to her old self.

"That's the second time this week that a Swanson has accused me of being crazy, and I'm starting to resent it. I would really prefer a thank you instead."

"Thank you? You think I should *thank* you? What if you would have shot one of those men? Do you realize the trouble you would be in?"

"No one was gonna get shot Teresa."

"How can you be so sure? The gun could have gone off and someone might be dead now."

"That's not possible."

"Really? And why not?"

"Because I forgot to load it."

She looked at him in shock and he grinned.

Marcella started laughing then Teresa and Randy started and soon they had to pull over until all three were finished.

Enzo was waiting nervously for Marcella to return and also any word from Teresa. When the Fiat pulled up to the house he rushed out to meet it. Marcella and Teresa emerged, then Randy from the back seat. Enzo was relieved to see them, then angry.

"Marcella! Once again you have disobeyed my wishes! I expected your return much sooner and was worried sick! And you!" He was pointing to Randy. "Did I not tell you she was to show you the way and nothing more?!

Randy took a step back, raised his hands and said.

"Whoa! Slow down, sir. You must know better than me that the women in this family make up their own minds. I couldn't control them any better than you can."

Once Enzo heard this he knew Randy was right and again shifted his anger to Marcella.

"Please, Papa. Zia Teresa was in trouble and I could not just do nothing and come home."

"Enzo," Teresa interrupted, "the meeting was going badly and took a serious turn. I am grateful to Marcella and Randy for removing me from the Graso office. Their timing could not have been better."

No one saw any reason to go into too many details for Enzo and Sofia's sakes. There was no need to frighten them any further.

Teresa and Randy left the cottage and walked up to the villa. It gave them some needed time to talk alone. As they walked side by side, Teresa slid her arm around his waist and he had to shorten his longer steps to match hers.

"I have missed you, Randy," she began. "I knew Tony did as well but he would never say it. He held on to his anger for many years. It became part of who he was."

"I noticed," he said. "When I first got to the ranch I couldn't reach him at all. I just couldn't break through the anger. It took some pretty drastic measures."

"I'm afraid to ask how drastic." She looked up at him and said, "He lost his father and the use of his legs in one terrible night. Then he pushed his brother away. He needs us now more than ever Randy, but he must learn to embrace life once again."

"I'm here for you both Teresa. Anything I can do to help just name it. I owe it not just to you and Tony but to Carl, too. He would have wanted me to watch over you two."

"I miss him desperately," she said, choking back her tears.

"That is why I had to come home. Everything in Texas reminded me that he was gone, and I couldn't bear it any longer."

"No one blames you for leaving, Teresa, not even Tony. We know how much you love this place, and seeing it for myself I'm beginning to understand why."

When they reached the villa Teresa took Randy's hand and said, "Come, I want to show something."

She brought him to the back of the house, up the back staircase, and onto the upstairs terrace. Together from this vantage point they looked out over the valley. The old tower in Siena could be seen in the distance.

"This was Pietro's favorite place. He never tired of looking out onto this land of ours. It gave him strength and a sense of belonging, as it does to me. That is why I fight so hard for it."

"No one will take it from you as long as I'm around Teresa."

It was a promise he intended to keep.

Chapter 28

Over his protests Teresa insisted that Randy take Pietro's room. The room had been unused for over a year now and it was high time someone slept in it. Marta put fresh linens on the bed and towels in the bathroom. The bathroom had two toilets, one normal-sized and one shorter, which he thought strange. He'd have to ask about that.

After a small meal he could no longer stay awake. Lack of sleep and the time change proved to be too much. He went to bed at seven o'clock that evening and slept straight through until five the next morning.

Once again his body clock proved to be the master. He got up showered and dressed. By then light was beginning show in the Eastern sky. He walked out onto Pietro's terrace. A slightly chilly breeze blew, even though it was early August, so he wrapped a blanket around his shoulders and sat outside. Soon he was witness to Pietro's favorite view. The sun crested the hills and lit up the valley. Randy wasn't prepared for this rush of beauty. "My God," he whispered to himself.

The smell of coffee drifted upstairs. He was looking forward to one of Teresa's morning cappuccinos, so he went downstairs to the kitchen and sure enough she was just starting to steam the milk.

"Good morning, Randy," she said with a broad smile.

"Mornin'. Just like old times," he said, smiling back.

"Keep your nose out of the foam."

"That takes all the fun out of it."

Teresa got serious now.

"I called Tony late last night to tell him you had arrived and about our little encounter with Roberto Graso and his man. I guess he knows you better than I because he was not the least bit surprised how you handled the situation. He does feel better knowing that you are here. Randy, I'm not certain what kind of impression you made in town yesterday, but I am sure it was not a good one."

"I think you're wrong about that. I'm pretty sure they'll think twice before trying to pull anything on the family, at least for a while. I scared the piss out them, literally," he said with a chuckle. "I think they're trying to figure out how far I'm willing to go and how they will deal with me. I am a new wrinkle they didn't plan for. One thing's for sure. I can't go around stickin' a gun in anybody's face that makes a threatening move, but I think I made my point so I won't have to. Let's take it a day at a time. They made their play and we made ours. Right now it's a Mexican Stand Off."

"A what?"

"It's when two cowboys have the drop on each other and one waits for the other to make a move. Don't you watch John Wayne movies? Everybody else around here seems to." They both chuckled and Teresa once again wiped his nose.

"What I would really like is to see this ranch of yours. When can I get a look at the stock?"

"Well, if you remember what we told you about way the ranch is run, the cattle are range fed, so they are quite spread out. We must saddle some horses if you want to see them. Unfortunately, I cannot go with you this morning. I have an appointment with my *avvocato*, my lawyer. I will see if Marcella is free to take you. She was looking down at her coffee but lifted her eyes to see his reaction to this suggestion. She saw his face blush a bit and a little smile appear. She thought he liked that idea just fine.

After calling Marcella, Teresa readied for her morning appointment.

"Keep your eyes open and don't get caught alone. Make sure you are always around people even if it's inconvenient. Okay?" Randy reminded her.

"I will. I should return for lunch." She kissed him on the cheek and left the house.

Randy met Marcella at the barn. Two horses had been saddled for them and after a quick double-check of the job, Randy mounted and Marcella did the same.

"Lead the way," he said.

"I always do," she answered with a smile.

"No doubt," he muttered under his breath.

They followed the well-traveled dirt service road around the ranch for a while before taking a trail that would bring them out to the range. The horses walked at a slow and steady pace. The morning sun was warming up, promising to turn hot as the day went on.

"So what do you do around here?" Randy asked. He was curious about her role in the ranch.

"Do you mean besides driving the getaway car?" Marcella said.

Randy laughed. "Yeah, besides that. Although, you *are* pretty good at that."

"Well, even though the Conti Ranch is mainly about cattle, the land also gives us much more — like wine grapes, hay, feed crops and olive oil. My interests are in the farming and the caring of the land, so I work with the farmers, planning crops, and with the vintners. What we don't use ourselves we bring to market. We have vineyard land around Montepulciano and Montalcino.

169

As you can see we have many hectares of olive trees in this area. Where we have no permanent crop we grow hay and rotate the fields.

"I went to the University of Siena and worked in the Oro Botanico there. That's the botanical garden that studies the indigenous plants and farming practices of Toscana. I learned much there about increasing our production with new farming methods.

"I have an office and a small apartment in town, but lately it has not been safe, so I have been staying with my family on the ranch."

"I'm hoping that after yesterday things will quiet down for a while at least," Randy said.

"I hope so, too, but I would not count on it. Come. I want to show you something." Marcella kicked her horse and sent it into a gallop. Randy followed close behind.

After a few hundred yards Marcella turned her horse off the main service road and down another cypress lined drive that was obviously much less traveled, with weeds growing in the tire ruts. About a quarter mile later they came to a large pond and beyond it a ruined villa. As the horses slowed and they came closer to the abandoned farmhouse, the view to the rolling hills below was breathtaking. The range stretched out for miles and the mountains to the east commanded the horizon. Randy did not realize it but he had held his breath. "What a sight!" he thought. "The view from Pietro's terrace was spectacular, but *this…*"

Marcella dismounted, tied off her horse to an old olive tree branch and walked toward the house. Randy did the same and the two of them stood on what was once the patio, the spot that commanded the best view.

"Zia Teresa and my father would play here when they were children," Marcella said.

"When she first came back after being gone so long, she would bring me here. We would pack a lunch, sit in the courtyard and practice my English. The pond is spring fed so the water is very cool even now in the middle of summer. You can swim here if you don't mind sharing it with the frogs and turtles."

"It's paradise compared to the muddy water holes I swam in back home in Texas."

With that, Randy began to undress. When Marcella saw what he was doing she turned away and pretended to further admire the view. She heard a big splash behind her.

"Woo! Hoo!" Randy yelled. "That water does have a chill to it! Feels great though! You comin' in?"

"No. I am not very hot and the water is too cold."

"You look pretty hot to me. You're sweatin' through your shirt. Come on! You won't be sorry! What's the matter, are you shy?"

That last statement sounded too much like a dare to Marcella and she was not one to back down from a dare. She stripped down to her bra and panties and ran for the water. Diving in, she swam towards the center of the pond where it was deepest and began to tread water.

Randy swam over to her. Her thick hair was wet and heavy falling straight back so that he saw her entire face. He drank in her beauty as he would the cool fresh water from this spring. Her full breasts were threatening to float out of the top of her bra and the cold water further enhanced their shape. He realized he was attracted to this woman like he had never been to another.

"Do you realize how lucky you are to live in this beautiful country?" he said, treading water a few feet away.

"There are times I get up and go to work as if it was any other day but very often I see something in this land that causes me to stop and truly recognize what it is that makes this such a special place. I know I could never leave it."

"Teresa left Tuscany to be with Carl." Randy said. "Until I came here I didn't realize how much she must have loved him. To leave her family and this land behind for the one she loved must have been an incredible sacrifice."

"Careful, Randy," Marcella smiled. "Toscana may be getting into your blood." She splashed him in the face laughing and swam to the edge of the pond.

She gathered up her clothes and ran for the ruined villa. She found a protected spot near the crumbling fireplace and began to dress. Suddenly, Randy appeared in the wide doorway wearing Hanks' Stetson and holding his clothes in one hand boots in the other. Marcella froze as Randy walked into the large empty room. Sunshine was streaming in through the missing tiles on the roof and dust was floating in the angled rays of light. Marcella's wet footprints on the brick floor in the dust led him right to her. He took off his hat, dropped his clothes and went to her. When he reached for her she did not resist. He ran his hands down her shoulders to her arms. He could feel the gooseflesh on her skin. Was it from the cold water or his touch? He filled his hands with hers and looked into those impossibly blue eyes. He kissed her deeply and she returned it in kind.

She pulled away from him and said.

"Do not allow your head to start something your heart cannot finish, Randy." She scooped up her clothes and ran to the next room. He let her go and did not follow. She was right. He did not want to confuse himself about why he was here and he also did not want to complicate his relationship with the Conti family. Hank would say, "Don't shit where you eat Randy."

"Good advice Hank," Randy said to himself, "Good advice."

He dressed quickly and went to the horses. Marcella came out a few moments later her hair still wet.

"I'm sorry Marcella. I think the beauty of this place and you must have gotten the best of me.

Marcella took his hand and smiled up to him.

"Do not worry about it Randy. I do like you very much and it was a beautiful kiss in my favorite place in the world. Someday I hope to make my home here. It was Zia Teresa's dream when she was young and now it is mine. I do not intend to make the same decision she made and leave my home, ever. Everything that I am is here on this land. You will leave to go back to your life in America. I have no illusions of moving away nor do I intend to let my heart be broken. It is best that we remain friends while you are here. Don't you agree?"

"I know you're right, Marcella. What you say makes perfect sense. I guess the problem is I don't really have much of a life in America anymore. I enjoy my work in Montana and I even still have thoughts of my ranch back in Texas, but since my father died my passion for it is gone. I envy you and your family that. All of you are willing to risk everything for your land and each other. Teresa's husband Carl once told me that her passion was contagious and that loving her opened his eyes to life. After coming here I finally see what he meant by that."

Marcella kissed him on the cheek and said.

"Come. Let us finish our ride. I want to introduce you to the Chianina." They mounted their horses and they left the old villa.

Once back onto the main service road they rode for several miles before it ended and became a horse and cattle trail. The land was now uncultivated and wild. Rocks and boulders that had been removed for centuries on the farms below were everywhere here. Even here in this rugged land the grasses and other plants were abundant. Soon they came upon small groups of cattle foraging on the drying grass.

As they got closer the cattle looked up to see who was coming but lost interest quickly and went back to eating, their favorite pastime. Randy dismounted and walked up to a large cow. She showed no fear of him so he spoke softly, stroking her large long face. He scratched her ear and walked around her to get a good look at the animal. This was such a relaxed and docile creature, unlike his Texas Brahman which could be nervous and jumpy, sometimes even unpredictable and dangerous. These animals were at peace with their surroundings. Hank always taught him to never turn his back on a bull due to its aggressive nature. In contrast, these large bulls were almost as quiet as the cows. There were only forty or fifty head in this group, but Marcella told him that it was not unusual for pockets like this to spread out over miles of range land. The *butteros* ride among the cattle to be sure they are free of disease and to provide assistance with calving if needed. They also spend time driving groups to more suitable grazing areas if they've cleared the one they were in.

Unlike the ranches in Texas and Montana where you might find thousands of head in one herd these small groups are very independent and require little supervision. Marcella told him the entire herd was less than three thousand and there were barely ten thousand head in all of Italy. That meant the Conti ranch had almost one third of the entire population of Chianina on the planet. No wonder some of the other families were so envious and wanted this land for their own.

It was getting hotter and close to lunchtime so they headed back to the villa. Randy was afraid that the kiss they shared back at the farmhouse might have made their new friendship awkward but it did not seem to. On the ride back she was cheerful and talkative.

"I have a meeting with some of our wine grape growers in Montepulciano tomorrow," Marcella said. "Would you care to join me? You must promise me to leave your big gun at home." She laughed.

"I would like that very much and I promise I will be unarmed." Randy laughed with her.

When they arrived back at the estate they said their goodbyes and Randy took the horses to the barn and handed them off to a ranch hand and thanked him.

He saw Teresa's car and knew she was back from her appointment in town and was relieved. It wasn't necessary to follow her around all day right now, but he wanted to be aware of her comings and goings just the same.

He went inside and found her in the kitchen preparing some lunch.

"Randy! Just in time for lunch. You must be hungry, yes?

"Very. Can I help?"

"Do you still remember how?"

"I'll have you know that back in Montana I am considered quite the chef thanks to you."

"Pardon me if I don't take that as too much of a compliment. It takes little skill to open a can of beans." She laughed and gave him a swat in the rear.

"Ha. Ha" Randy said. "My mushroom risotto just happens to be the best in Montana."

"That is because it's the *only* mushroom risotto in Montana!" She laughed again.

"Very funny." He faked hurt feelings.

"Seriously, Teresa, you taught me well and I paid attention. The guys back at the ranch literally cried when I left."

"Those were tears of joy, Randy." This time she doubled over with laughter and he did the same.

They talked while they made lunch together like they used to. He missed these conversations so much. They helped him get through the time after Hank's death and they felt warm and familiar now. Teresa was the female influence he had missed out on all of his life. She filled the void he sometimes felt with love and kindness that only a mother could. He may have not felt that he needed a mother when he was younger but that did not mean he did not want one.

After the lunch plates were cleared they sat at the table with some cool sparkling water.

"I did something today that I shouldn't have done."

"Who did you shoot Randy?"

"Wow! The hits just keep on comin'!"

"I'm sorry. What did you do?"

"I kissed Marcella."

"Where?"

"On the lips where do think?"

"No silly, where were you?"

"At the old farmhouse by the pond. We went swimming and I got a little carried away."

"That is an easy place to get carried away. There is much beauty there."

"That's just what I said. She kissed me back then pushed me away. She knows I will eventually be going home and she thinks I will break her heart."

"Well you are a heartbreaker Randy."

"I'm serious. I really like her Teresa and don't want to hurt her, but I can't help the way I feel."

"Sometimes you must do what is best for others, Randy; respect their wishes and put your own feelings aside, especially if you really care for them. *Capisco?*"

"Capisco."

Chapter 29

After breakfast the next morning Randy heard a car horn honking from the drive. He went out and saw Marcella standing next to the Fiat waiting impatiently. "*Andiamo!* Let's go, Cowboy!" she yelled from the car.

To this point Randy had only seen her dressed only in jeans and boots. Now here she was dressed for her business meeting in a form fitted dress that showed off her figure. With her higher heeled shoes she presented a statuesque almost model like appearance. Her hair was pulled back revealing her high cheekbones and smooth olive skin with just a hint of make up that highlighted those incredible aquamarine eyes.

Randy had never seen a more beautiful woman and was at a loss for words as he approached her. He went straight to the little Fiat and got in but had to take off his Stetson to fit into the tiny car. He looked over to Marcella and smiled.

"Not much headroom in these things."

"We do not wear big cowboy hats in Italy." Marcella smiled back.

"That's what's wrong with Italy. No sense of style."

She sped down the dirt road in her usual way and pulled onto the main highway.

"Montepulciano is not far, only 30 minutes. You will love it. It is a small but beautiful little hill town; the highest in Toscana. There is much wine there, some of the best in Italy. I have a meeting with the growers that should not last too long. Then I will show you around the town."

"Great," Randy said, but he could not take his mind off of the kiss they shared yesterday. Neither one of them noticed the car following them.

They left the highway and started on the road to the hill town, passing wineries and tasting rooms along the way.

"We grow grapes that go into many wines in the area. Mainly Sangiovese for Chianti but some vintners have been experimenting with new blends using French Bordeaux wines like Cabernet Franc and Merlot so we have only recently planted some of those vines. They grow well and we will have fruit this year."

"All I know about wine is what Teresa has taught me," Randy said.

"Then you had a good teacher."

The road to the village got steeper and steeper. Soon they were high above the valley. Since cars were not allowed in the upper village they parked in a lower lot and walked up the hill.

"The grower's office is in the old village and I must go now or I will be late. Feel free to wander the streets and I will meet you back here in one hour." She pecked him on the cheek and left him standing near the railing.

At a bench overlooking the patchwork fields below, Randy sat down and took in the view. From this high vantage point the whole valley stretched before him. The blue sky still had a bit of morning haze as the light fog slowly burned off. The air was slightly humid but so fresh that Randy wanted to breathe in more than his lungs could hold. It was still early so there were very few people out and the stores and tratorrias had not yet opened. He decided to explore while Marcella was busy working.

Randy stood and as he turned he found two men standing in front of him. One he recognized immediately even though he was wearing a black fedora and dark glasses. The other larger man was obviously hired muscle.

"Buongiorno, Signore John Wayne."

"If you are looking for the restroom I think they are near the parking lot. Wouldn't want to see you have an accident," Randy said sarcastically.

The man produced a .38 caliber revolver from his coat.

"I don't think I will be the one having the accident signore. Come with us where we can have a more private conversation." The larger man frisked him, shook his head at the man with the gun then motioned in the direction of an old stone warehouse at the end of the railing. They came to a small door and Randy was directed to open it. Randy complied because the man with the gun always gets to make the rules. He stepped through the door and stood aside while the larger man entered. Then the mustached man crossed the threshold. His gun hand was extended and as soon as Randy saw it he quickly drove his shoulder into the thick door and slammed it on his arm as hard as he could. There was an audible crack as the man's arm broke in the heavy old doorway. As he screamed and dropped the gun Randy picked it up and pointed at the hired muscle. The large man froze in his tracks.

"Parli Inglese?" Randi said, but the thug just shook his head with frightened eyes. Randy pointed to the floor and ordered, "*Siediti!*" The big man immediately dropped down on the dusty stone floor. Meanwhile, the mustached man kneeled in the open doorway, moaning and holding his broken arm. Randy grabbed him by the back of his jacket and dragged him into the room next to his hired man.

"This is becoming a real bad habit," Randy said to him. "What's your name? *Qual è il tuo nome?*" The man did not answer so Randy kicked him in the ribs with the point of his boot and he yelled out.

"That's why we call them shit kickers," Randy said. "What is your name mister?" he repeated.

"Nunzio," the man said through gritting teeth.

"Well, Nunzio. I guess you did not take me very seriously at our last meeting. If this is going to keep happening I think will have to just shoot the both of you right now. The two men spoke in Italian to each other and the big man cried,

"*Si prega di non spararmi Signore John Wayne! Per favore!* Please don't shoot me Mr. John Wayne! Please!"

"*Fouri!* Get out!" Randy yelled and motioned with the pistol to the door. The big man scurried out like a rat without looking back, while Nunzio remained on the dusty floor.

"So, Nunzio, should I just shoot you now?"

"I am hoping you do not." Sweat was beading up on his forehead even though it was cool and dark in the warehouse.

"I can understand that. It would look very bad for you if you got shot with your own gun. That's too bad because I came here with a friend and she asked me to leave mine at home so I guess this one is going to have to do." Randy pointed the gun at Nunzio's head and pulled back the hammer.

"Arrivederchi, Nunzio."

Nunzio held his good hand up to Randy.

"Don't shoot signore please!"

"Why shouldn't I? You have caused me and the Conti family a lot of trouble for a long time, Nunzio. I told you to stay away from us and yet here you are trying to kill me."

"We were not going to kill you signore, just rough you up a little and hope you would go away."

"That does not make me like you any better, Nunzio. You are a coward and a man with no honor, a killer of bulls, a slapper of women and you enjoy running helpless people off the road. Not to mention you wet your pants. Your own mother would thank me for killing you!" Randy was yelling at him now. "Tell me, what do I have to do to get Graso off our backs?"

"Kill him," Nunzio said, dead serious.

"I was hoping for something a little more diplomatic. I promised Signora Conti I would try not to kill anyone but you people are making it very hard for me to keep that promise. Get out before I change my mind."

Nunzio slowly pulled himself up and walked to the door. His dark clothes were covered in ancient dirt and dust that he did not bother to brush away.

"I am adding your gun to my collection. I'm sure you understand."

Nunzio said nothing and just left quietly cradling his broken arm.

When Marcella returned Randy was standing near the car.

"Unlock the car, please."

She did as he asked and he pulled the gun from his waistband, slid it under the seat and locked it back up again. When he looked up Marcella was staring at him like a mother would look at her child for disobeying her wishes.

"I thought you were not bringing a gun today, Randy," she said firmly.

"That's not my gun. I took it from the man we saw in Graso's office and I had to break his arm to get it so I'm keeping it."

"What did I miss?"

Randy explained to Marcella how his morning had gone. At first she was silent. She wasn't used to this kind of violence and it took her a few minutes to process Randy's story.

"How can you be so calm about this Randy? Two men just tried to kill you! *Per l'amor di Dio!* For the love of God!

"He said he only wanted to beat me up and send me home but I have no reason to trust anything he says. I've never killed anyone in my life, Marcella, and I hope I never have to, but these men keep pushing me to my limit and I'm afraid something may happen if they don't back off. If I keep letting these guys go they're going to know that I don't want to kill and may see this as weakness. At least they are focusing their attention on me and not the rest of the family. I can handle myself."

Randy reached out to her shaking hands and held them.

"It's over for now, Marcella. I am not going to let this spoil my time here with you. Show me the village."

The cobblestone streets of Montepulciano are very steep, and most of the shops and restaurants lay along the *Corso*, or main street, heading uphill. Once they reach the Piazza Grande, the Palazzo Comunale or town hall, commands the square with its all seeing clock tower and fortress-like facade.

Marcella stopped and sat on the steps of the old church, Santa Maria delle Grazia, with Randy next to her. From this vantage point they could see the whole square. The piazza was quiet today with only a few tourists taking pictures around the town's historic community well. But Marcella tells him this piazza hosts many festivals and events so is often very crowded.

"This place has been here since the days before Christ. It was also once an old Roman garrison and was fought over many times. First ruled by Siena and finally by the Medici in Florence, now it is famous for its wine, agriculture and of course its beauty," Marcella said.

"There's so much history here." Randy responded. "Where I'm from a building is considered historical if it's a hundred years old. Here that's a blink of an eye compared to these ancient churches and towers."

"Perhaps you are beginning to understand why our traditions are so dear to us and why we are so tied to our lands. We live in the same homes generation after generation. Families have friendships or hold grudges that can last many lifetimes. We are constantly reminded of our history and the achievements of our forefathers because we are surrounded by it every day." Marcella stood and held out both her hands to Randy.

"Come. Let's eat and taste a little wine before we leave."

Randy took her hands and she pulled him up as he pretended to resist and forced her to pull harder. Finally he rose and they stood close. He was once again drawn to her. He could smell her hair as a light breeze blew it about her face and he resisted the urge to brush it aside and kiss her. Their eyes connected in recognition of the moment and the mutual attraction. She broke the spell and looked away.

"Come, I am starving," she said.

They walked back down the hilly street to a small trattoria. Bright colorful umbrellas shaded the tables outside. The ancient street was so steep that the tables and chairs had to be placed on raised platforms to make them level. Randy ordered a cold Peroni in a chilled and sweating glass. That beer was perhaps the most refreshing he had ever tasted.

As they were talking quietly there was a sudden crash in the street and they both jumped with a start. A small pile of rubble appeared on the cobblestones that was not there a moment ago. A piece of the building's facade had just chosen that moment to let go and fall to the street below.

"You must be careful around here or a piece of history may land on your head," Marcella laughed.

After lunch she took him to a small wine tasting room in the back of the restaurant. They tasted a few Vino Nobiles that Montepulciano is famous for along with some Brunellos from Montalcino. These were much more sophisticated than the simple Chianti Randy was used to. The higher quality wine was a nice discovery for him. Most of these were made from the Sangeovese grapes grown in Conti vineyards. They brought a few bottles with them for Teresa.

On the way home Marcella had forgotten about Randy's encounter with Graso's men and was in a pleasant mood.

"You have come to Siena at a very good time Randy. We are celebrating the Assumption of the Virgin Mary next week, a very holy event for us. It was on this day that Mary rose to Heaven, body and soul, after her death. With that celebration come many events and feasts. The most exciting in Italia is The Palio di Siena."

"I've heard a lot people talking about that since I have been here but don't know what it is exactly. It's a horse race, right?"

"Not just a horse race but the greatest horse race in all of Toscana. They lay sand and clay soil in the Piazza di Campo and race around the piazza. There are seventeen *contrade*, or how you say, neighborhoods, in the city of Siena. Each *contrade* has the opportunity to race but only ten are chosen. It is a great spectacle and thousands will be there. It is only days away." Randy could hear the excitement in her voice.

"Sounds like the Kentucky Derby Italian style. I'm looking forward to it."

After the short drive back to the villa, Marcella dropped Randy off with his wine gifts for Teresa.

"Do not forget your new gun, Cowboy. You may need it."

"I hope not." Randy said as he tucked the weapon into his waistband. Then he went to find Teresa to fill her in on the events of the day.

Chapter 30

After spending the afternoon in the hospital, Nunzio Salvatore, his fresh white plaster arm cast in a sling tucked under his coat, now sat in Roberto Graso's office.

Graso slammed his fist on his antique desk.

"This American cowboy is making a fool of you Nunzio and because you cannot take care of him I also look the fool!" he screamed. "Since Teresa Conti's return she has succeeded in not only strengthening the Conti holdings but has rallied many of the other families to her side! The Societa degli Agricoltori della Valdichiana are meeting next week to decide the future of Chianina ranching in Italy. I am running out of time and I am *tired* of your bungling!"

"She has no reason to fear us, Signore Graso. She is not alone any longer and does not fear for her own safety. She values her lands more than her own life."

"If we cannot break her then you must kill her *and* that meddling cowboy before the meeting takes place. Do you think you can manage that, Nunzio? Because if you cannot I must find someone who can and you may find yourself on that list as well."

"It will be done Signore Graso, I assure you."

"See that it is."

Chapter 31

Randy woke early as usual. He packed a few things in a small travel bag and went downstairs to have coffee with Teresa.

"*Buongiorno,* Randy," she said as she handed him his coffee. Noticing the bag she said, "Going somewhere?"

"A few of the hands are going out into the hills to bring in some strays. I want to go with them to get to know how things are done here. It's just for one night so I won't need much. I'll be back by tomorrow afternoon. What are your plans for today?" He did not want to sound overly protective but after what happened in the village yesterday he wanted her to be careful.

"I am just going to work in the study today and get caught up on some business."

"Good. I was hoping you would say something like that. I really didn't want you to go into Siena today while I was gone. I don't think Nunzio will bother us for while with that broken arm of his but there is no telling what Graso is up to."

"I am unaccustomed to having a bodyguard Randy but I must admit I feel much safer when you are near." She gave him a motherly peck on the cheek. "I hope you enjoy your campout *mio figlio*, my son. I will be fine here."

Randy gulped his coffee and headed out to the barn. The three other *butteros* were saddled and ready. They had Randy's horse saddled as well but as usual he checked the cinches himself.

"*Andiamo.* Let's go." He said and they rode out into the Tuscan dawn.

Only one of the three men, Matteo, spoke any English and not very much at that. Randy's Italian was improving but only a little. If he wanted to get better he'd have to find a tutor. Meanwhile he got by with what little he picked up along the way.

For the first few miles he said nothing, just listened to the men as they spoke softly in Italian to each other. They spoke in low voices as though they did not wish to disturb the birds and animals so early in the morning. A light coating of dew covered the ground and kept the dust down on the trail, which smelled of damp earth. As the four men rode westward, the dark sky grew lighter and the sun struggled to break the night's grip on the *Val di Chiana*, The Chiana (Kee-ah-na) Valley. Soon the sky brightened from starry black to an intense blue even though the sun hadn't yet crested the mountains. Matteo pointed to them, waving his hand from left to right, and said, *"Montagnas di Appennine,* The Appennine Mountains." They extended down the spine of Italy from the far north to the far south. Deep green patches of forest higher up the hillside contrasted against the lower rolling and dryer foothills.

The land they were riding on had become more rugged and grassy with fewer trees. They began to see signs of the herd and it was plain to see that it had grazed here. Chianinas are eating machines. They constantly forage in search of more grass, and now that late summer was here they had strayed further eastward in their never ending quest for food. Often they would go higher where the grass was still green and the *butteros* had to search them out to bring them down to the valley before the weather turned too cold in the mountains.

Small groups of cattle were gathering and the men rode among them on horseback, stopping every now and then to examine a calf or an injury that may need attention. The cattle, demonstrating the quiet and amiable nature of the Chianina, only showed vague interest in the cowboys. After a quick inspection the men continued on. The cattle became fewer and soon the search began in earnest. The men found a hilltop so they could see far across the valley and used binoculars to seek out the strays that had wandered too far. They spotted a few right away. Randy understood Matteo for the most part when he explained that they would split up along the perimeter of this part of the valley and drive any strays down to a chosen spot below.

Randy headed northwest at a slow trot. The thought crossed his mind that he was alone in Italy for the first time since he had arrived. Yet he felt completely at home here on this open range. It was familiar territory even though he was thousands of miles from home. This could be Montana, Colorado or Wyoming. The job was the same, really, and it was a job he was born to do. With all the uncertainties in his life this was one of the few things he was sure of. He loved this life as much as Hank did. Randy was sure his father would be proud of what he was doing and that he had taught his son how to do this job well.

After only a mile or so Randy spotted a cow and calf foraging on a hillside. The calf was still showing the red color it was born with, but it was fading to the gray it would become. He went around them, and with some whistles and yells he got them headed downward. When he was sure they would continue in the right direction he rode on. He would come back this way to be sure. After several hours of climbing over the rocky

190

terrain and driving a dozen or so of the big Chianina cattle downward he back-tracked and herded them all to the meeting place on the valley floor. The big cows were slow but steady in their pace and by late afternoon as the hot summer sun started to cool he reached the rendezvous point.

Matteo was already there with about sixteen head and one of the other men was coming in with eight more. The last man was not yet there.

"*Molto bene,* Randy! Very good!" Matteo yelled. "You have done well!"

"*Grazie* Matteo! You have not done too badly yourself!"

The last man came into view now, and as he neared, Matteo rode out to him and helped him trot in the last ten strays.

"*Quarantasei!* Forty six! A good day's work!" Matteo said with a big grin.

"We will keep them together here for the night and join them with the rest of the herd tomorrow."

He spoke to the other men and they both rode up into the scrub brush. In a few minutes they returned with a load of firewood each. Matteo circled some stones and stacked some of the wood in the center. While he was doing this the rest of the men removed the saddles, bed rolls, and water from each horse. One of the men produced a large dented metal bowl, and with it he watered the horses. Matteo brought his bag over to the fire pit and showed Randy what he had brought: some large grain rice, a small onion, garlic, Chicken bouillon, dried mushrooms, dried herbs, and hard pecorino cheese.

"Risotto? Out here?" Randy said, surprised.

"Si!" Matteo said, smiling as he started to work. By the time the sun had gone down over hills to the west, the fire had died down enough for the cast iron pan and small pot of water to go into the coals. Matteo heated some olive oil and sautéed the rice, along with the garlic and onion. As he added hot bouillon to the mixture, a wonderful smelling cloud of steam rose from the fire. He continued adding liquid, and when he was satisfied the rice was almost perfect he added the herbs and mushrooms. Finally the cheese was folded in and the risotto was ready.

Old chipped enamel metal plates and coffee cups were passed out and one of the men opened a bottle of Chianti. As the last of the sunlight faded, and the four cowboys enjoyed their risotto and wine by the campfire. "Sure beats hot dogs with canned pork and beans," Randy thought to himself. They raised their glasses to Matteo and toasted his cooking skill.

Each of the men took a two hour watch to be sure the cattle didn't wander off. Randy took the first watch and left the others at the fire to talk freely in Italian without worrying about him. They were all in high spirits and laughed at each others' stories. He took his cup of wine and walked among the cattle. They were down for the night after another grueling day of wandering the hills in search of food. He was beginning to feel affection for these animals that he had never felt in all his years working with cattle. They had a stoic and majestic presence about them. Maybe it was their large size or their quiet deliberate movements but mostly they just seemed at peace with the world and he was envious of that.

The fresh night air seemed to flow all the way from the sea just to cool him down. In Texas it stayed hot and humid through the night. The Gulf of Mexico didn't care for his comfort and dared him to sleep in her warm and damp blanket. In contrast, the cool Mediterranean thanked him for his service and granted him a night's rest so he could serve the land the next day.

His watch was over, and as he lay in his bedroll a feeling of gratitude came over him. Randy felt grateful to be right here, right now. The incidents that brought him here were both terrible and wonderful. Without them he would not have come to be here with these people in this place. How many nights had he laid awake wondering how his life would be different if he could erase some of those events—leave the good and take away the painful. The truth was every one of those life altering experiences brought him to this place and time. Even if he could go back and change the smallest tragedy it would set him on a new course. He would not be the man he was and he would not be here now. Fate was just a word a few weeks ago, but it carried a much stronger meaning now as he lay under the moonless night sky in Tuscany, five thousand miles from Texas.

The four men woke at first light. Each had some coffee and a small bread roll with olive oil, just enough to keep them going until they got back. The cattle were waking and were starting to move about. The men saddled up and packed their bedrolls. It would be an easy task to keep the cows moving at a steady pace all the way to where the rest of the herd was gathered. The sun was rising and it promised to bring another hot Tuscan summer day.

The sounds they made to keep the cattle moving were different for each man. Each had his own style.

"Heeyea!" yelled one man.

"Andiamo! Andiamo!" said another. The last man just had a loud whistle and waved his rope wildly. Randy did a combination of both a high pitched whistle and "Let's go! Let's go!" Together they kept the cows' short attention span focused on the task of moving forward.

The man bringing up the rear started to sing a familiar song. His voice was a loud and deep baritone. It reminded Randy of an opera Teresa took him and Tony to in Houston once. *Rigoletto* he thought it was. He remembered the humpbacked jester in the play singing this same song. He was too young to appreciate it then but now as he heard the *butterro* singing the song it seemed to fit well with the small cattle drive they were on. But it sure would raise some eyebrows if he were driving the herd in Montana.

As midmorning approached, Matteo told Randy he knew of a spring nearby. They could rest there and water the cattle and horses. They shifted the small herd just a bit southward until they came to a grassy green area with a small pond surrounded by shady trees. The men had no trouble bringing the herd to the water. As the animals drank their fill, the men rested in the shade of the trees out of the August sun. Randy pulled his straw rancher's hat over his eyes and half dozed while listening to the men chatter. The drone of their voices and the soft cool grass under him combined to make him drowsy, and he drifted into a deep sleep....

Hank was sweating in the sun working on the windmill near the barn. There had been no water from the well for two days. Randy handed him a big pipe wrench. It was heavy in his small hands.

"That should do it Randy!" He started the windmill spinning and went to the pump.

"Pump the handle, Randy, as fast as you can!"

Randy was pumping now. Up, down, up, down.

"Faster, Randy! Faster!

Suddenly water burst from the spout. Randy was still pumping. Hank took off his hat and stuck his head under the cool water. He came up smiling broadly and splashed water in Randy's face.

"Nice job Randy!" Hank patted him on the back.

The Texas cowboy woke from his short nap while the images of the dream still lingered. Randy smiled at the memory of that hot day in Texas as his dream faded. The men were getting back on their horses and Randy rose to join them. The cattle were reluctant to leave the water and tasty green grass. They took a little prodding but soon they were moving again.

The sun was getting serious now and threatened to bake them in their saddles. At last they caught sight of the larger herd and drove the cattle toward it. With one last push from the cowboys, each in his own way, the cattle moved to rejoin the herd, slowly mingling in until they disappeared among the others and went back to grazing.

"Buon lavoro! Good job!" Matteo yelled to the men. The four headed for home. They were hot and hungry and eager to get cleaned up after two days on the trail.

Randy saw the weed-covered drive that led to the old farmhouse. The urge to go for a swim in the cool water was stronger than his hunger. He waved to the men and kicked his horse into a gallop as he rode past the tall straight cypress trees, shadowless in the high noonday sun. When he reached the pond he dismounted, tying his horse to the same old olive tree he had the last time when he was here with Marcella. He couldn't get his clothes off fast enough.

He dove out towards the center of the pond and felt refreshed as the cool spring water shocked his hot skin. The splash sent a few green turtles basking in the sun to the dark safety of the bottom of the pond. Randy treaded water for a few minutes, then rolled over and floated on his back. With his eyes closed and his ears submerged the only sound he heard was his own breath. He couldn't remember the last time he felt this much at peace.

"Hey! Cowboy! You are trespassing!" Marcella's voice broke the silence.

He snapped his head up to see her still on her horse at the edge of the water.

"Are you going to call for the *carabinieri?* The police?" Randy yelled back at her, smiling.

"No. I think I can handle you myself," she said as she got down from her horse. She took off her clothes, all of them this time and dove toward Randy in the middle of the pond. When she reached him she wrapped both arms around his neck and kissed him.

"I was just thinking of you," Randy said, as he stared into her deep blue eyes.

"I can tell," she answered, smiling and looking sheepishly down and under the water. Randy returned a knowing grin.

"I was at the barn when Matteo returned. I brought you something to eat."

"Suddenly, I'm not so hungry." Randy said, and he kissed her again.

Treading water was difficult as they held each other and they both went under. They came back to the surface, laughing, and swam for the edge. The sun struck their bare skin just to remind them who still ruled the day.

Gathering their clothes, they ran for the farmhouse. Randy spread his jeans and shirt out on the dusty clay tiled floor, laying on them as he pulled Marcella to him. As he ran his hands across her body, her wet flesh only added to his desire. He followed the curve of her back to the firmness of her buttocks and with his hands full, he pulled her closer against him. It was not enough to kiss her. He needed to press his body so close that there would be no space between them.

"I will not break your heart, Marcella." Randy heard the promise made come from his own lips.

"Do not make promises you cannot keep, Randy," she said into his ear.

Randy's lips were exploring her neck while his hands explored her body. She was smooth and muscular. He cupped her full firm breasts that were still cold from the swim. Her dark nipples were hard and erect. She moved forward and he took them into his mouth, circling them with his tongue. She moaned and reached between his legs and took him into her hands.

Then it was he who moaned as she gently stroked him. Her wet hair was heavy and cold on his chest and he shivered as the cool droplets of water fell, running down his sides to the dusty clay tiles to form muddy pools on the floor.

She still had him in her firm hand and guided him to her wet warmth. As he entered her they both exhaled with pleasure. She fell back on him slowly until she could go no further. As she began to rock he rose to meet her. A slow rhythmic dance began as they moved against each other. She rose up, back straight and he

197

saw her beauty in its entirety. Full heavy breasts rested slightly on her ribcage. Her stomach was flat but fleshy with a wisp of a dark hairline that faded into her thicker darker hair below.

Marcella took his hand and guided it to the place she wanted to be touched. A loud moan let him know that he had found it. He circled the spot with the tip of his finger and her rocking began anew. It was he who must stay in control then. If it were up to him he would have simply given in to the building sensation he knew was inevitable but he must wait for her. It was his gift to her for being there with him at that moment in that beautiful place.

Marcella rocked faster now and her deep breaths were keeping time with her motion. Randy knew her time was near. He saw it in the flush of her face and her half lidded eyes. Suddenly she pushed hard against him and threw her head back splashing him with droplets of water from her wet hair. The vein on her neck was full and bulging with blood. A loud "*Oohhh!*" escaped her lips against her will. Her muscles tensed and she was a marble statue in their rigid contraction.

Now he wanted to join her ecstasy and sped his rhythm, not caring when the moment would come because he would give in to it immediately and fully. There was no reason to hold back now. When his moment arrived he let it take him. The release started at his core and spread outward throughout his torso. His orgasm radiated toward the edge as a burning coal sends heat from its white hot center. He felt himself flow like never before with powerful rapid throbs that slowed as his orgasm began to subside.

Marcella fell forward and laid on him, breathing heavily. He could feel her firm breasts on his chest and it excited him once again. She whispered in his ear.

"Not bad for a Texas cowboy."

"I would have to put you right up there in the top ten myself," Randy whispered back.

With that Marcella drove her elbow into his ribs hard and Randy had to defend himself against a flurry of slaps and punches. They laughed and rolled on the dusty brick floor until Randy emerged on top, pinning her arms to the now muddy floor. He leaned in and kissed her deeply. In that moment Randy realized he was in the arms of the great love of his life.

After a quick dip in the pond to rinse off the dirt and dust, Randy and Marcella dressed, sat under the old olive tree on the grass, and ate what she had brought. Salami, cheese, big green olives and fresh bread were spread out on a large cloth napkin on the grass. Randy was ravenous and ate quickly, not even waiting to swallow before he shoved more food into his mouth.

"Leave some for me, *Cinghiale*!" Marcella laughed.

"Teresa used to call me that too," Randy said with his mouth full.

"That's because you eat like one!"

Randy stole the bread from her hand and stuffed it in his already full mouth.

"Hey!" she yelled, giving him another barrage of slaps.

After lunch Randy was lying on the grass with Marcella's head on his lap.

"This is such a beautiful place Marcella. Why has no one fixed the house and chosen to live here?"

"It takes much work and great expense to restore these old villas Randy. You must really love a place to

199

do what is necessary to bring it back to life. I would do it if I had the money. I want to have a family here one day."

Randy was falling in love with this place, this woman and this land.

On the ride back to the villa, Marcella said.

"Randy, would you like to take a little trip with me tomorrow?"

"No."

"What?" Marcella sounded insulted.

Randy laughed and she hit him hard in the ribs again.

"Okay, okay. I'll go if you insist. My ribs can't take another punch. It seems like everyone wants to beat me up these days."

"It must be your Texas charm," she said, and she whacked him again.

"I would like you to experience a traditional Chianina steak dinner. In Cortona, tomorrow is the start of the La Sagra della Bistecca. It is a celebration in the Gardens of Perterre, the main park in the town. They grill the Bistecca Fiorentina for three days over a huge wood fired grill. If you want to learn about the beef here, this is something you cannot miss.

"Sounds great. I always love a good barbeque. Is it an overnight trip?"

"Do not get your hopes up, Cowboy."

Chapter 32

The next morning Randy called Tony back in Calvert. It would be late in the evening there, but Tony had always been a night owl anyway and would be up.

"Randy! Good to hear from you, Brother. I understand you are handling things with your usual smoothness. Glad to know that you decided to keep a low profile and not piss anyone off there in Italy," Tony said with his famous sarcasm.

"It was your idea to send me here Tony. If you wanted smooth you should come yourself, and you've got some nerve accusing me of pissing people off. You wrote the book on that," Randy joked back. He told him about the incident with Nunzio in Montepulciano. "You were right when you said these guys are playin' hardball, Tony."

"Watch your back, Brother. You're the only thing standing between them and Mom." Tony's voice was laced with worry.

"I can handle it, Tony. I won't let anything happen to Mom.

He changed the subject.

"Hey, I met a girl, Tony. She's like no one I've ever known. I think I'm falling in love with her. She's as smart as she is beautiful. She has an edge to her though, stubborn like Teresa. Must run in the family."

"What are you going to do when you come home, Randy? Will she come back with you?"

"I couldn't ask her to do that. She is a Conti through and through. You know how this family feels about their land. Remember how much your mom missed her home all those years? How it tore her up inside? Since

I've been here I've learned how much she really gave up for you and your dad, to leave this place and to stay away so long. I couldn't do that to Marcella. I won't."

"I have some news for you, too, Randy and I really need to talk to Mom about it. There's a big ranching conglomerate buying up a lot of land here in Calvert. They're paying top dollar, too. You know I'm no rancher and Mom has her hands full there. I think we should entertain an offer for the ranch if it comes. Mom would probably agree."

"What would you do then, Tony?" Randy asked.

"I've talked to Mom about going back to Houston or even Dallas to start using my God given talents in the business world. I have the credentials and I know I have what it takes Randy. I just need someone who'll give me a shot and let me prove it."

"You don't have to prove anything to me, Brother. I've known it since we first met. Think about coming here for awhile Tony. Teresa could really use your help with the business. She may be in over her head and I know you could straighten out the finances so she could concentrate on the ranch."

"We'll see what happens with this ranch first. Then I'll decide what to do next," Tony said. "You have some decisions to make yourself, Randy. With me gone there won't be anyone here to watch out for your place. I know you've been avoiding that choice, but you're going to have to work it or let it go."

"Yeah, I know, believe me, but right now, it's the least of my worries and I'll cross that bridge when I come to it."

"Just keep it in mind Randy. You may not get another chance like this for a long time."

They talked for awhile longer about nothing, really; each was just happy listening to the other's voice. Then Randy said goodbye and hung up. He knew Tony was right. He'd been avoiding that decision since the day Hank died. His father put all he had into his five hundred acres; it was everything to him. To let it go would be to close that chapter of his life forever. Hank would become nothing but a memory. Already it was hard to picture his face sometimes. There would be nothing tangible left of him in this world, just what was in Randy's heart. He couldn't see working the ranch without Hank. It had always been the two of them together, and it just wouldn't be the same doing it alone. He would be reminded every day that Hank was gone.

Deep down Randy also knew that Hank kept his own soul, that he was a man apart from the rest of the world. Maybe the war did that to him or that was just who he was and maybe that's why he lost the woman he loved. Randy did not want to become what Hank was, a man alone except for the son who idolized him. Possibly that was the greatest lesson of all that Hank could have taught him.

"Don't be like me, Randy. Hold on to the people you love." Randy almost heard Hank's voice but he was sure it was his own conscience talking.

For the last seven years he had been living like his father, keeping to himself and not letting anyone get too close. But since coming here he had opened his heart. He was a changed man and he knew it. He must decide what to do with his ranch soon, but today Marcella was coming to take him to Cortona.

Chapter 33

Marcella decided to take Randy the long way to Cortona, off the main highway along the winding roads that led through the high hills. The vineyards and wineries were in full swing preparing for the harvest. The olives were ripening in the summer sun and would be ready for picking in October. It was a busy time in Toscana, but this was also the week of the Assumption and many went on vacation to the sea to escape the heat of August.

It was a time for feasts and festivals celebrating the Virgin Mary and her rise to Heaven. Since so many were on holiday elsewhere, traffic on the curvy roads was light except for a few tourists or bicyclists taking mysterious pleasure in climbing these steep country roads. Perhaps the thrilling ride down was worth the torturous climb.

They continued to rise higher and higher and every so often were granted a spectacular view of the valley below through the pine trees. Finally they reached the top of the hilly range and began the slow descent back down to the valley floor. Many small towns dotted this side of the hills. Some homes clung precariously to the steep slope, but most preferred the convenience of living in nearby towns. Once the car reached the flat, straight roads out of the hills, Marcella picked up speed and raced along the straightaway, so they made much better time.

Soon they reached the busy modern town of Camucia and they had only to drive up the steep and narrow road up to the ancient walled village of Cortona. They parked the Fiat just below the gate and walked up the sharp angled cobblestone street. The climb was a little strenuous but mercifully short.

Just past the quaint entrance to the Hotel San Michele the narrow street opened up onto the Piazza della Republica. As is in Siena and Montepulciano the old town hall over shadowed the piazza. The fortress-like clock and bell tower was the tallest building, with a long wide stone staircase used primarily as a gathering place to sit and watch the people mill about the piazza. Children ran up and down the chipped stone steps, chasing one another or stopping to eat gelato that quickly melted in their sticky hands. Several young couples at the farthest and highest corners of the steps were holding hands and stealing an occasional kiss.

On the corner, a fruit and vegetable market sold the bountiful harvest of Toscana. Boxes of colorful produce lay stacked in front of the store and Marcella bought a large bunch of juicy ripe green grapes. They climbed halfway up the steps, sat on the warm stone, nibbled grapes from a brown paper bag and watched the people passing below. Most are tourists as they could tell by their Bermuda shorts, floppy hats and cameras hanging around their necks or by the giant shopping bags bulging with souvenirs.

Directly across from the steps on the other side of the piazza, elderly villagers sat on benches and enjoyed the highlight of their day: watching the colorfully dressed tourists and talking among themselves. Some were ignoring the crowd and were sewing or reading the paper talking over the news of the day. Being seen in the *piazza* was just as important as seeing everyone else. One old gentleman might spot an interesting character among the tourists; he would whisper in his friend's ear and both would roar with toothless laughter. Randy's

Stetson and boots would surely draw attention from these old guardians of Cortona.

The sun was still high and it was too hot to sit on the steps for long. Randy and Marcella made their way to the cool shade of the Via Nationale, the shaded narrow street that is the center of shopping and dining for the tourists and locals alike. There trattorias and outdoor cafes were packed with patrons enjoying an afternoon meal or a cool drink.

The shops were laden with food and wares from all over Italy. Hand painted ceramics and figurines from Deruta, knick knacks, paintings, wines, cheeses, salami and olive oils tempted passers-by. The aroma of fresh breads, garlic and basil poured out the doors of the trattorias onto the street. The wonderful smells blended together to form one great Tuscan temptation to the senses.

Randy wanted a cold beer so they sat at a small table out of the sun and ordered drinks. Now *they* became the watchers and the crowded street gave them plenty to see. Randy heard many languages being spoken at once, even the occasional and familiar English.

"Like most of these hill towns, Cortona was founded by the Etruscans over two thousand years ago and has been built on since then," Marcella explained.

The town's atmosphere was medieval and modern at the same time. Most of the interiors of the shops and restaurants had been updated while the exteriors remained as they were in the past. Randy saw this blending of centuries throughout Tuscany. The old and the new existed at the same time, unlike back home where it was common to tear down the old and start from scratch. While the Italians cherished their history and did whatever possible to preserve it, even at great cost, Americans often did what made the most economic sense, even if it meant the loss of a grand structure that had witnessed their short but colorful history unfold.

As the sun fell in the sky, the late afternoon brought shade and with it a pleasant temperature to the village. More people ventured from their homes where they had been avoiding the heat of the day. The piazza was busier than ever and the narrow streets were now overcrowded.

"Let's go to the park now. I am getting very hungry," Marcella said.

They paid their check and walked the short distance to Gardens of Perterre. As they strolled Randy reached for Marcella's hand and squeezed it gently. He was rewarded for his touch with a smile and a kiss on the cheek. The street opened onto the Piazzale Garibaldi with its monument to the great Italian General. Marcella guided Randy to the balustrade at the edge of the piazza. From this vantage point he could see clear across the Val di Chiana. Marcella pointed to the huge lake on the far side of the valley.

"That's Lake Trasimeno. It is just outside of Toscana in Umbria."

"Beautiful," Randy said but he was no longer looking at the view. Instead his gaze was fixed on her. As she turned to him he looked into her eyes and knew he was lost. As a soft warm breeze rose up from the valley her dark hair danced about her face. He brushed it aside and held it in place behind her neck. As he leaned down she met his lips and they shared a tender kiss. Randy heard or saw nothing else, only this woman whom he had only just met. But in that short time he knew he would want no other woman more.

As their lips parted and as they opened their eyes, they saw only each other. Marcella gave him a smile he had not seen before. She had given in to him and this smile betrayed her secret. Randy knew she loved him now and a joy rose from his chest making his eyes water and lumping his throat. He held her tightly until the intense emotion passed and he could speak.

"How about that steak?" he said with a grin.

Marcella was shocked! She looked at him with round eyes and her mouth hung open.

"That is not what I expected to hear you say at this moment, Cowboy!"

She started to punch him but he caught her hand and kissed her once more.

As they reached the park the sun had set but lights had been strung all around. The canopy of trees was now the ceiling and the grass the carpet. Tables had been set up throughout the park and they were filling up fast. The couple paid for their dinner in advance, and Marcella pulled Randy over to the cooking area.

A dozen men stood around the gigantic fifty-foot grill, tending to the fire or turning thick t-bone steaks. Randy had never seen such steaks! They must have weighed over three pounds each! Some were so thick the chefs had to stand them upright sideways on-edge so they cooked properly. The grillers used long metal rods with hooks to constantly turn the meat, preventing it from burning in the hot sizzling fire.

Each man was responsible for a certain group of steaks. As some steaks were ready and removed, another man threw fresh meat on the grill to replace it. The assembly-line process relied on a well disciplined army of fire tenders and grillers. The massive grill was roped off so onlookers didn't get too close and interfere or get injured. Meanwhile, a large crowd gathered outside the rope to watch or to take pictures.

"Come. Let's get a table while we can." Marcella took Randy's hand and hurried to the center of the park. They found two seats at a table near the stage where a small band composed of a piano, electric guitar, a stand up bass and a drummer was playing Italian songs. The piano player had a clear deep baritone voice that rose above the noisy crowd.

As they sat at a long table with the other diners, Randy shook hands and smiled while Marcella made introductions. Everyone seemed fascinated with the American cowboy having dinner with them on that warm summer evening. They smiled and joked in Italian, making index-finger-and-thumb pistols as they pretended to shoot one another. Once again the Great John Wayne was invoked and Randy laughed at the mention of his name.

The waiter came to the table to take orders for side dishes, and a short time later two giant medium rare steaks arrived, along with side orders, a bottle of Cortona Chianti, and a cold bottle of water each.

Randy had been looking forward to this steak since that night in Texas when Carl first spoke of it so many years ago. He was not shy and so cut himself a large piece, one big enough to fill half his mouth. He held it there for a moment, taking in the flavor and aroma and appreciating it as only a Texas cattleman could. The steak was tender and delicious, one of the most flavorful pieces of meat he had ever tasted, with a naturally rich and savory essence that was juicy but not fatty and needed nothing more than the bit of salt with which it was seasoned. Carl was right. This could very well be the best steak in the world.

This dinner meant more to him than most; he was sure of that. So many desires and dreams were to be realized with this wonderful steak. This is what the Swansons wanted to bring to America. This is what started it all and ultimately brought him here to Tuscany. It was a simple meal enjoyed all over Italy, but it had the power to change his life forever.

"What do you think of your steak Randy?" Marcella wondered.

"It was worth the wait," was all he said, and he dug into it with a vengeance.

To his surprise he had no problem finishing the huge meal along with fresh tomatoes with basil, a peach, and half a bottle of wine. Marcella barely ate half and he eyed her leftovers hungrily.

"You have certainly earned your nickname today *Cinghiale*! I cannot believe you have eaten all of that food." Marcella laughed at his powerful appetite.

After the plates were cleared they sat and enjoyed the wine. They had another bottle but dared not open it if they were to drive home.

The music was softer now and the diners were full and sleepy. Marcella turned to Randy and said,

"Zia Teresa tells me you are a guitar player. Yes?"

"I play a little sometimes at the ranch in Montana. It passes the time on those long winter nights without a woman." Randy joked.

"Would you play something for me tonight?"

"Here? Now? I don't think that's a good idea Marcella. I haven't played an electric guitar since high school.

"Please you must!" Marcella stood and stepped over to the small stage. She whispered in the piano player's ear and he smiled widely. She returned to her seat laughing.

"What did you tell him?" Randy was nervous now and with good reason.

Just then the man stood and spoke loudly into the microphone. Randy only caught a few words but knew he was about to be put on the spot. Then he heard:

"*Famosa Americana cantante e chitarrista* Randy Bartlett!" Famous American singer and guitar player. Now Marcella laughed as she clapped along with the rest of the crowd in the park, prodding and pushing him towards the stage. Somebody handed Randy an old beat-up Stratocaster and he reluctantly hung the strap around his neck. He spoke a few words to the musicians and they all smiled and nodded enthusiastically, as he started playing his fathers favorite song "Hey Good Lookin'" By Hank Williams and sang into the microphone.

"Hey Hey Good Lookin', what you got cookin'?
How's about cookin' somethin' up with me!
Hey sweet baby, Don't ya mean maybe?
We could find us a brand new recipe!

As he played and sang he looked out into the park. The people had awakened from their after dinner drowsiness and were clapping along. Some of the teenagers danced on the grass and the adults and children alike joined in.

Randy struggled a little to remember the lyrics of the song and made some mistakes but no one seemed to notice. They probably didn't know the words anyway, so he ad-libbed when he got into trouble. Even though he hadn't played the song in many years he played it well enough and was having fun. The small combo played along with him and appreciated the impromptu jam session.

Marcella was dancing with a smiling young boy on the grass and would look up every now then and laugh. Randy saw her and had to concentrate so he didn't laugh when they made eye contact.

As the song wound down to the last four bars, the small band stayed with him right to the end and when they struck the final chord they stopped perfectly together as though they had rehearsed the song many times before.

The audience in the park erupted in applause and cheers. A few were yelling, "Bravo! Bravo!"

Randy took off his Stetson and took a big bow then waved it at the band as the crowd clapped for them as well. He shook each of their hands and stepped down from the stage into Marcella's arms. She was trying to kiss him and laugh at the same time so Randy got mostly a mouthful of teeth as a reward for his musicianship.

"That was wonderful Randy!"

"Thanks but I'm still mad at you for putting me on the spot like that," he said, but didn't really mean it.

"Please do not be angry Randy. See? Cortona loves you as much as I do!"

As she said those words she wrapped both arms around his neck and kissed him as the audience applauded them both for their tender expression of love.

As the couple left the park and wound their way back through the narrow streets Marcella said, "Let's stay here tonight Randy. Do you want to?" Randy paused for a minute as if to consider the question and received a poke in the ribs for his joke.

"I would like that very much, Marcella."

"That is better. We will go to the Hotel San Michele and see if they have a room for us. Then we can pick up a few things for the night."

They checked into the hotel and Randy called Teresa to let her know they would not be back tonight so she wouldn't worry. They returned to the street and found the *tabacchi*, a small store that sells cigarettes, bus tickets and essential toiletries. They got just what they needed for a one night stay. The wine store was close so they bought a bottle of chilled *Prosecco* to take back to the room.

After returning to the hotel Randy stood on the terrace looking out over the Val di Chiana. Night had drawn its dark curtain over the valley and lights twinkled across the now black landscape. The larger towns appeared as heavier concentrations of lights and the headlights of moving cars wound through the night on the rambling roads around Cortona. Randy heard faint music rising from the street below, as somewhere the day's festivities were not yet over for some. Now the couple eagerly anticipated the pop of the wine bottle as Marcella opened the chilled champagne-like Prosecco.

She joined him on the terrace, handing him a glass of the sparkling wine. They touched their glasses together and took a sip. It was delicious.

"So many wonderful discoveries since I have been here," Randy told her. "Teresa once said to me, sometimes you never know what you are missing until someone shows you." He wrapped an arm around Marcella's waist and pulled her close. "You have shown me so much in so many ways, Marcella. Most of all how alone I have been all these years. You have filled an emptiness I didn't even realize was there, and now that you have I can never go back to the man I was. I am in love with you Marcella but of course you already knew that."

"I knew, but still I wanted to hear it from your own lips. I love you too, Randy, more than I can say. That is why I know that you will not be able to keep your promise not to break my heart." As she spoke her voice cracked and her eyes filled. A tear from each eye spilled onto her cheeks and Randy kissed them away before they fell. He brought his tear-salted lips to hers and the sadness of their love merged with the joy, for the two are never really far apart.

She pulled him inside and to the bed. As she lay down Randy laid down beside her. He touched her face and looked as far into her eyes as he dared without drowning.

They took their time and did not let desire overcome their passion. They touched, kissed and explored each other. This was not as much about sex or even lovemaking as much as it was about not missing a moment or place on their bodies. This time together must never be forgotten. No matter what happened after this night Randy and Marcella would always cherish the Tuscan summer night when they professed their love for one another and demonstrated it the best that they could, by giving each other pleasure.

Hours passed and even though they fought it as long as they could, sleep finally took them both. They lay in each other's arms all night. Even as they slept they could not let go.

The glorious morning sun poured through the terrace window and Randy woke as the light struck his

214

face. Marcella was still sleeping when he rose and went out onto the terrace. Already there was activity in the village. What he did not see he could hear and smell. Coffee was brewing, breakfast meats were sizzling, eggs were being fried, and bread was being toasted. Small trucks buzzed about below, bringing fresh supplies to the stores and trattorias. Voices rose to the terrace from the piazza as men and women began their daily labors. Morning is a busy time in Cortona, and it was quickly slipping away.

Dressing quickly, he left in search of the hotel's breakfast room to find coffee to bring to Marcella. The continental breakfast was just being laid out for the guests, so he filled twos cups, adding a little cream and sugar to both, then stole a tray to load up fruits, cheeses, and pastry. As he made his way back to the room, bed headed guests began to emerge with the same purpose in mind.

When he let himself back in, Randy found Marcella sitting up in bed but with her eyes closed letting the morning sun that streamed from the large terrace window warm her face. As she heard him enter she opened her eyes and smiled warmly.

"Buongiorno signore. Grazie!" she said as he placed the tray on the bed table. Randy got undressed again, joined her in the bed and they picked over the tray of food he brought. As she sipped her coffee she eyed him, watching him eat with his usual enthusiasm.

"Tell me about your ranch in Texas and your life there." She looked at him in such a loving way that he was compelled to tell her anything she wanted to know.

"It doesn't look like much now but I have so many great memories there working with my dad. It was ours and anything we put into it was for us alone, good or bad. I have seen how the Conti family cherishes their lands and it was much the same for us. But we were two men alone and we depended on one another for everything. If Hank had lived I'd still be there.

"We were more than father and son. We were partners and best friends." Randy had not spoken of Hank like this for many years and was surprised his grief was still this close to the surface. He did not speak for a few moments and Marcella let him take the time he needed to continue.

"Now the ranch is all I have left of him and I just can't let it go." He spoke the words out loud for the first time that he had been keeping to himself.

"Would I like Texas, Randy?" He knew what she was suggesting and he felt elated but he knew it was selfish to allow this idea to go any further.

"I could not ask that of you Marcella. Not after seeing how connected you are to Toscana, your family and your home." He reached out his hand and touched her face.

"Do you not want me to be with you?" Tears were falling on her cheeks and Randy wiped them with his hand.

"More than anything, but I saw how much Teresa missed her home and I will not watch you suffer the same way she did because of me."

"Is it better that I stay here and suffer a broken heart when you leave?" She was crying openly now and Randy held her close.

"Please, Marcella let's not talk about this now. I'm still here and we are together that's all I want to think about." He kissed her all over her face then laid her back down on the pillows and kissed even more deeply. How could he leave this woman after she has given him so much? Randy once again heard the voice of his father: *"Hang on to the ones you love with both hands, Randy, and never let go."*

On the drive back to Siena they were in a somber mood. A dark sadness hung in the car with them and it overshadowed the wonderful time they had spent together in Cortona. When they pulled up to the villa, Marcella shut off the motor and turned to Randy.

"I am sorry for spoiling our lovely time Randy. From now on I will enjoy our time together no matter how long that is. The Palio begins tomorrow and it will be great fun. I promise."

Chapter 34

Marcella took a back way into the city, escorting Randy and Teresa to the Palio in her tiny Fiat. There would be thousands of people in Siena today and all the main streets would be inaccessible.

"My apartment has a small parking garage so we can leave the car and walk to the Piazza di Campo from there."

As they approached the oldest sections of the city the streets became narrower. Marcella zig-zagged through the tight spaces at reckless speeds. The side mirrors of the car seemed inches away from the high stone walls as she raced down one street then turned sharply down another, seemingly at random.

"Jesus Christ, Marcella!" Randy screamed.

"What?" she said calmly.

Teresa wasn't at all bothered by Marcella's driving.

Just then, as they emerged from a confined alleyway into a busy intersection, a bus appeared on their right and honked its ear splitting horn. Marcella stomped on the gas pedal and rocketed through, just ahead of the bus. The tires squealed as she made the sharp turn.

The force of the circular motion slammed Randy hard against the car door. He looked at her with wide eyes, mouth agape, but she didn't notice, as she was concentrating on her driving. She shifted gears often, but used the brakes sparingly. Finally, whipping into a narrow opening, Marcella pulled inside the small dark garage, slammed on the brakes and came to a stop inches from the stone wall in front of them. As she shut off the engine the only sound was the ticking of the hot motor as it cooled and the thudding of Randy's beating heart as he tried to catch his breath.

"What is the matter Randy?"

He just looked at her and said. "Nothing Marcella. Nothing at all." He was already dreading the ride home.

Now, as they walked the streets of Siena, Teresa and Marcella took turns pointing out places of interest to Randy. The city was packed with tourists and locals alike, all here for the great spectacle of the Palio di Siena.

The closer they got to the Piazza di Campo the heavier the crowd got. Soon it was difficult to navigate the streets because of all the people. The three held hands so they wouldn't get separated. Bright colorful flags flew everywhere. At last, they reached the piazza and Randy felt as though he'd stepped into an ancient arena. The noise from the crowd was deafening. The tall old buildings held the sound in and rose into one gigantic roar of voices. The piazza is shell-shaped, like a scallop, and a fence had been constructed at its center to form an uneven track at the perimeter. Tens of thousands of people filled the center of the track. Dirt had been brought in by the truckload to create a racetrack covering the stone pavers underneath.

Normally the seats were sold out a year in advance, but one of the vintners Marcella worked with arranged seating for them in the bleachers that have been set up for the race.

"Our seats are near The Fonte Gaia, The Gaia Fountain." Marcella pulled Randy in the direction of the fountain, directly across from the fortress-like Palazzo Communale, the town hall and the Torre del Mangia, the great tower that rules the Siena skyline. Teresa followed. A sea of people stood between the fountain and the tower with just the dirt track exposed. The rest of the space was consumed by the spectators cheering and waving the colorful flags.

Randy tried to stop and admire the fountain but Marcella pulled him along. Its waters were cool and inviting on this hot summer day. He wished he were one of the pigeons resting on the heads of the she wolf statues that spouted cool water from their mouths. The birds occasionally took a drink and shook the water from their ruffled feathers.

Marcella waved to someone in the bleachers. The man saw her and waved back, guiding them to their seats.

"This way!" Marcella said to Randy as she pulled him up the bleacher steps.

Marcella reached their host and kissed him on both cheeks, introducing Randy and Teresa as well. The high vantage point in the bleachers allowed them to observe the entire piazza. "It sure pays to know the right people," Randy thought to himself.

As they sat the two women explained the great race to Randy.

"The Palio is at the very heart of the Sienese people. Everyone in the city lives for the events every year. There is one on July 2 and this one August 16," Teresa explained.

"The seventeen *contrade* or districts of the city are represented on the flags. Do you see?" Randy looked at the colorful flags and noticed the pictures of a dragon, an owl, dolphin, goose, seashell, tower, unicorn, tree, giraffe, tortoise, panther, porcupine, eagle, snail, she wolf, caterpillar and ram. Each had its own set of colors.

"Oh, I see." Randy nodded.

"Each symbol and its colors signify the *contrade*. There is great pride for your district and some rivalries have lasted hundreds of years. There are allies and enemies among them. Some will conspire to see that an enemy *contrade* does not win the race. Cheating is always suspected and must be guarded against.

"Only ten can race so the seven that did not will get to race the next time and lots are drawn for the three remaining open spots."

"The winner of the race takes the *Drappellone* home to their *contrade*. It is a beautiful banner that is especially created by a different artist each year for that Palio. No two are alike. It will hang in their district church for all to see and take pride in."

"How much money do they win?" Randy asked Teresa.

"There is no prize money. Only the honor of winning and of course the bragging rights."

Now Marcella told him, "There are some *contrade* that have not won a Palio in many years. The longest without a win is called *Nonna*, Grandmother, and the desire to lose that nickname is very strong. *Bruco,* the Caterpillar, is now the *Nonna* and wants the win badly. Since we live outside the city we do not belong to a *contrade* but we like to cheer for the *Nonna*."

"I always root for the underdog myself." Randy said.

The August sun finally fell low enough for the aged stone buildings to cast a cool shadow on the Piazza di Campo. The mass of people no longer stood in the hot sun and all were relieved for the shade. Tuscan summers can be glorious but also oppressively hot, especially if you are standing in the center of a breezeless Italian piazza shoulder to shoulder exposed to the sun's piercing rays.

Suddenly the crowd grew louder at the far end of the piazza from the direction of the Duomo. A squad of *carabineri* on horseback, and in full dress uniform entered the piazza and began a slow walk on the track. Their swords were drawn as they rode with their backs straight and in perfect formation. Once they completed the lap they stopped. They held out their swords and broke into a full galloping charge. The crowd cheered the mounted police as they raced one lap around the track, charging an unseen enemy. Randy imagined a long-ago battle with this courageous cavalry galloping across the field of honor slashing at the enemy with their swords. As they exited the piazza the crowd applauded them wildly. While the throng still cheered Randy heard horns and drums and a parade began to appear on the track.

"Now comes the *Corteo Storico*." Teresa said loudly over the growing noise. "It is the great parade."

The colorfully dressed pages carried the flags of the *contrade* beside the archers and soldiers. Everyone was marching in escort of the *contrade* representatives themselves. The marchers wore full renaissance dress and armor, as they slowly marched in step with the beat of the drummers and trumpeters. Flag throwers tossed their bright silk banners into the waning summer sky, catching them with skilled dexterity.

After the nearly hour-long procession Randy saw four huge Chianina bulls pulling a cart, escorted by soldiers and knights on foot. Now Marcella told him, "That is the *Carroccio* it carries the *Drappellone*, the banner that will go to the winner."

As the chariot made its way around the track, the bell in the great tower, the Torre del Mangia, rang out over the piazza.

Randy was more interested in the enormous bull oxen hauling the heavy wooden cart. Even with more than a dozen people on board the bulls pulled the cart easily and effortlessly. Their black crown-like horns emerged from their long faces, and as a team Randy knew this was an easy task for these giants.

Chianina are the greatest work animals in history and were the earth movers and tractors of their time. These powerful creatures were instrumental in the building of this great city and every other Renaissance town in Italy. While most everyone in the piazza cheered for the *Drappellone*, the great prized silk banner of the Palio, Randy quietly paid homage to the Chianina bulls and their ancestors. The respect he felt for this breed on the open Tuscan range had now doubled as he watched them pass, and he felt honored to be in their presence.

The horses and barebacked riders now appeared on the track and presented themselves to the people by slowly taking three laps around the piazza. The crowd was delirious and the sound that came from them was nearly enough to bring down the old buildings bordering the track. A loud explosion rang out and Randy jumped from the unexpected noise.

Teresa told him that this meant the race was about to start.

A heavy rope was stretched across the track and nine of the ten bareback riders struggled into position behind it. Then another was raised behind them and horses were now between the two ropes. They were having difficulty keeping the horses in line as some refused to remain. The race could not begin if any horse was not in its proper position. The tenth horse lagged some distance behind the rope and finally when the signal was given he began galloping toward the line. The rope dropped as the running horse reached the line and the other riders kicked their horses into a gallop. The greatest horserace in Italy was on!

The throng of spectators roared in unison. As the horses reached the first turn the leaders set the pace. The speed of the racers increased, and when they reached the second turn one horse slipped in the loose soil and spilled his rider onto the track. The horse recovered and continued to run with the others, leaving the rider behind. Randy was told even if a horse loses his rider he can still win the race.

When the pack reached the straightaway Randy saw some of the jockeys pushing each other. Some were hitting other riders and horses with their riding crops. This type of interference was allowed, even encouraged, and the crowd screamed at the sight of the intense competition. Some cried foul but knew it was an empty objection.

A sharp and treacherous turn came up, but the horses did not slow as they reached it. Two collided at full gallop as one slammed into the padded wall and fell along with his rider. There was a collective breath drawn across the piazza, but the other riders did not stop for the fallen man. The pack raced on at full speed.

The first lap was completed and the steeds fought for position of the inside lane. One emerged and desperately tried to hang on to his narrow lead while the others charged on behind him. Once again they reached the tight and perilous turn and once more there was a frightening collision of men and horses. Another fell to the track, throwing dirt high into air. Already the stones beneath the soil were becoming exposed, bringing increased danger to the remaining group.

Hooves thundered on as the horses reached the fastest part of the track. Now was the time to make their move and they all knew it. The jockeys drove their beasts to the limit and some began to close the gap on the leader. The group reached the third lap and the final push began.

The masses shouted out for their chosen rider and horse, in hopes that their roaring support would give them strength and aid in their victory. Randy looked over at Teresa and Marcella and they too were caught up in the excitement, screaming and cheering on the riders.

The deadly turn came once more but this time all horses kept their footing. The two front horses were so close that Randy could not tell which was the leader. The crowd was on its feet and all eyes were on the leaders. As the third and final lap ended, one horse lurched in front of his challenger and crossed the finish line inches ahead. *Selva*, The Forest was the winner! Pandemonium reigned as the spectators poured onto the track. Green and orange flags with its tree symbol dominated all others. Men embraced each other and some raised their arms praising God for his wisdom in granting the win, while others cursed him for making the wrong choice. Men and women alike shed tears of both joy and disappointment. The revelers swarmed the Selva *contrade* horse and jockey just to lay hands on them.

The race that had taken months of preparation, thousands of hours of work and planning, was over in less than two minutes. The winning horse and jockey pressed their way through the growing tide of joyous Sienese people in the direction of the Duomo.

"They go now to the Duomo for the *de Deum*, the prayer of thanks," Teresa shouted above the din. "We should make our way out of the piazza while we can!"

Marcella thanked the man that supplied the seats that gave them such a magnificent view of the race. Now the three made their way through the crowd, going against the tide of people heading for the great cathedral.

There standing outside a bar bordering the piazza, Randy saw the familiar shape of Nunzio Salvatore leaning against the stone wall smoking a cigarette, his new white plaster cast visible under his black coat. Nunzio noticed Randy and the women as well. He reached up with his left hand and touched the brim of his fedora. The two men eyed each other warily but neither could do anything about this unexpected encounter in public. Randy did not tell Teresa or Marcella and they continued to push through the crowd of celebrants.

When they reached Marcella's place they decided to go upstairs and have a cool drink in the air conditioned apartment. She unlocked the door and they entered the stuffy room. Marcella opened the windows to let out the hot stale air and turned on the air conditioner. After a few minutes she closed the windows and the unit took over to cool the small space.

While Marcella and Teresa prepared the drinks and snacks Randy headed for the bathroom. Again he was faced with the two toilet dilemma. As usual he elected to use the larger but still was confused about the purpose of the smaller. After washing his hands and splashing cool water on his face he emerged from the bathroom, went into the small kitchen, and asked the women, "Why is it that you need two toilets?" His tone expressed his curiosity. Teresa and Marcella looked at each other and suddenly burst into hysterical laughter. They held each other so as not to fall because they were both unsteady and their legs weakened. Tears flowed from their eyes and as they wiped them they tried to compose themselves.

"What's so funny?" Randy asked. Between chuckles and giggles, the two women explained to Randy the second "toilet" was actually a bidet. He blushed as they described the appliance and suggested he give it a try. Coming from a family that did not even make an indoor toilet a priority this was a custom that would take some getting used to.

Marcella saw his embarrassment and mercifully changed the subject.

"Let us go outside for the sunset."

She had a small rooftop terrace and the three took their drinks and went to watch the setting summer sun. The orange sunset blended softly with the red tile roofs and warm yellow stone buildings of Siena. It was as though they were wearing tinted glasses and saw the whole world bathed in the golden light. As the glow faded the air became cooler and a light damp breeze rose above the city.

"Autumn will be here soon. I can smell it in the air," Teresa said softly. A slight sadness resonated in her voice, as though she were already mourning the loss of summer.

The Palio represented the last of the season and now that it had passed the hard work of harvesting its fruits and preparing for winter would begin.

Chapter 35

Nunzio Salavtore was once again in the office of his employer Roberto Graso.

"I have discovered the cowboy's weakness, Signore Graso, and I intend to use it against him very soon."

"What might that be?" Graso eyed him with doubt. So far Nunzio had been unable to deal with this meddling American from Texas or that bitch Teresa Conti, and his confidence in the man was greatly shaken.

"The young Conti woman, Marcella." Nunzio said. "He is obviously taken with her."

"As are many young men in Siena, even my own son," Graso said. "How does this help us?"

"I have seen him unable or unwilling to follow through with his threats against us. I do not believe he is the killer he wants us to believe he is. I think he will back down if Signorina Conti is threatened."

"It will take more than threats, Nunzio."

"Si, Signore Graso, it will."

Randy was in the barn with Teresa and a few of the *butteros*. Six new horses had arrived and they were inspecting the livestock.

"Most of our horses are from Maremmano stock," Teresa told Randy. "They have been here in Toscana since the time of the Etruscans, more than two thousand years. Back then the horse was smaller but very strong. It was also a very skittish horse and difficult to control. They have been bred with English thoroughbreds for the last hundred years and are now larger and gentler. They do not tire easily, so our men like them on the range. We also have some Tolfetano mares as well. They too are an old Etruscan breed, strong and tough, very good for herding the cattle."

As they were examining the horses Enzo came into the barn looking for Teresa. He was visibly shaken which was unusual for this stout Italian man. Obviously excited, he needed to speak with her right away.

"Teresa. I have a letter you must read from the Societa degli Agricltori Valdichiana." He handed the letter to Teresa. As she read the letter she too became noticeably agitated.

"What is it?" Randy asked Teresa.

"There is a meeting to be held in Arezzo next week. All the major cattle ranchers are asked to attend. The Americans are interested in our Chianina and want to start a breeding program to bring our cattle to the United States."

Randy was shocked! This is exactly what Carl and Teresa tried to do over eight years ago! Now after all that had happened since then they were now finally considering doing the same.

Teresa continued, "Apparently the largest producers and land owners have a say in the decision since they have the most to lose or gain. The larger the producer the more power they will have in influencing the change in policy. Now we know why Graso has been so aggressive lately. He must have known about this meeting for some time now. If he had control of the Conti Ranch combined with his own, he would be able to use his power to prevent this from happening and could keep the status quo and manipulate the beef prices as well."

Teresa spoke firmly now.

"Carl would have wanted this breeding program to be successful. I must see to it that it comes to pass."

Randy said to Teresa, "I am more worried about Graso right now. I know his type. If he feels cornered and believes he could lose power or control he may do something desperate or dangerous. I want everyone to be extra cautious until this meeting is over. Don't leave the ranch alone under any circumstances and only when absolutely necessary."

Randy turned to Enzo and asked, "Enzo, where is Marcella?"

"She went to San Gimignano this morning to meet with the Vernaccia growers. The quality of the vines has fallen off for many years and she is helping to restore them," he answered.

Randy did not like hearing this news at all. As long as she was with the growers she was probably safe, but he hated the idea that she was traveling alone. He said only to Enzo, "Let me know when she returns or even calls. I just want to know she is safe."

"I will, Randy. Do you think she could be in any danger?"

"I'm sure she is fine, Enzo, I just want to keep close tabs on everyone, that's all." Randy said it, but he didn't believe it. He would not feel right until Marcella was back safely on the ranch. Enzo went home and Teresa and Randy returned to the villa.

Hours passed and still there was no word from Marcella. He tried not to show it but he could not stop worrying about her. He prayed she would at least call so he could hear her voice. The thought of her in trouble kept creeping into his mind and he could not block it out. From upstairs he heard the phone ring and his heart almost jumped out of his chest. Teresa answered it as he was racing down the stairs.

"Randy!" Teresa screamed.

He was already there and saw her holding the phone with a look of horror on her face. She handed it to him as soon as he reached her. As he brought the receiver to his ear he heard a familiar voice.

"Signore John Wayne? Are you there?"

Nunzio Salvatore was on the line.

Randy took a deep breath to compose himself. He did not want to sound as frightened as he felt.

"What do you want, Nunzio?" Randy sounded detached and in control, almost annoyed that Nunzio was interrupting his day.

"Buongiorno, Cowboy. I trust you are enjoying this fine weather."

"You didn't call to discuss the weather, so I repeat. What do you want?"

"I am calling to suggest you and Signora Conti take a little drive together on this lovely day to San Gimignano. There is someone here who would enjoy your company very much."

"Randy?" Marcella came on the line, her voice faint, strained, and shaking.

"Marcella? Are you alright?" Now the panic in his voice could not be hidden.

Nunzio came back on.

"Listen carefully Cowboy. Go to the Pallazo Comunale and the *museo,* museum. It is closed today but the back door will be open. Find the entrance to the Torre Grossa, and climb the stairs to the top. We will be waiting for you in the bell tower. If you do not come or I see any *polizia* I will open her throat as I did that abomination of a half-breed bull of yours." The line went dead and Randy stood frozen with the phone to his ear. He looked over at Teresa and she was staring at him, waiting to hear what was happening.

231

"He has Marcella."

"Lode e Dio! Oh my God! Teresa gasped. She brought her hands up and covered her open mouth and still stared at him with fearful eyes.

"What does he want Randy?"

"Us." Randy said. His mind ran wild searching for a way out of this crisis.

"He wants us to come to San Gimignano and I think he means to kill us there."

"What do we do?" Teresa started to panic now as she tried to wrap her mind around these events, but logic was rejecting them as not real, not possible.

"The only thing we *can* do Teresa. We must kill him first." Deep down Randy always knew it would come to this.

"I've had two chances to do that and I didn't. Now he has Marcella. If anything happens to her I will never forgive myself for not killing that bastard when I should have." Randy was suddenly overcome with guilt. Had he shot Nunzio in that dusty warehouse Marcella would not be in danger today. But he couldn't dwell on that now. He had to get her back.

"This is not your fault, Randy. You cannot blame yourself." Teresa reached up to him put her hands on his face and forced him to look into her eyes.

"Carl's accident was not my fault either Teresa, but it would not have happened it weren't for me. The same is true now. Why do the people I love always have to suffer for my mistakes?" He could not help himself. Years of guilt and self punishment had caught up with him all at once. He wrapped his arms around Teresa and wept.

"I am so sorry, Mom!"

He heard himself speak the words to Teresa for the first time; declaring her to be his mother. In this time of crisis and self recrimination he needed his mother like never before. Teresa was the only mother he'd ever known and he loved her for filling the emptiness in his life. His own mother left him behind, but Teresa was always there for him. From now on, he would let nothing or no one hurt the two women he loved, even at the cost of his own life.

Randy suddenly released Teresa and stood resolutely straight. Now that he had decided to kill or die trying to rescue Marcella, he would plan accordingly.

He went upstairs with Teresa close behind. From his drawer he removed the two pistols, Hank's Colt .45 and Nunzio's .38 Smith and Wesson. He filled the clip of the .45 and pushed the magazine into the grip; safety on, with no shell in the chamber. He had removed the bullets from the .38 when he first put it away so now he reloaded it. There were only six shells.

Teresa watched him as he methodically loaded the weapons. The fact that he was preparing to use them was frightening her even more.

"Are you going to kill him Randy?" She asked.

"No. You are."

"*What?!*" She screamed at him." I have never shot a gun in my life! I do not know how!"

"You are about to learn." Randy said. He shoved the .45 into his waistband and held the .38 in his hand. With his free hand he took Teresa's and led her outside, ignoring her protests.

Randy guided her to a stand of trees facing away from the villa. He now did for Teresa what Hank had done for him as a boy, showing her how to use a pistol.

233

He stood behind her with his hands over hers. They held the revolver out together. Randy released the safety, thumbed the hammer and pulled it back. The cylinder turned with a metallic click then stopped as the hammer locked. A round was now in the chamber and waited only for the trigger to be pulled to send the bullet on its course.

"See that tree just ahead?"

Teresa nodded without speaking.

Randy continued, "I expect us to be very close to him. That's very good for us. That tree is less than ten feet away. If we are this close or closer you cannot miss. Just point it at him and pull the trigger. *Capisco*?"

She nodded again.

"When I pull my hands away I want you to count to three then shoot." As Randy released his grip, the gun was in her hands alone and it started to shake. He put his hands back on and the shaking stopped.

"Easy now, steady. Take a deep breath."

Her chest rose as she slowly breathed in, and as she released the breath he freed her hands once more. The gun no longer shook and she was calm.

"Now count to three and squeeze the trigger straight back." Teresa counted.

"Uno, Due, ..."

Just before she reached the third count she closed her eyes tightly.

"Stop," Randy ordered. "Don't close your eyes. You must see what you are shooting at or you will miss. Start again."

"Uno, Due, Tre."

Teresa fired the weapon. She held tight to the grip so the recoil was not too bad. Only a small jolt traveled up her arms to her shoulders. As soon as the shot was fired splinters from the tree bark and trunk flew through the air.

"All right now. Here's what we're going to do."

Randy told Teresa his plan.

The drive to San Gimignano only took thirty minutes, and there was still a few hours of daylight left. The road leading to the old village wound slowly up the hill. Bucolic vineyards surrounded him but Randy did not see their beauty. He only looked straight ahead and feared for the woman he loved. He feared for himself as well. Not for the loss of his life. That he was ready to sacrifice if necessary without question. He was most afraid of living if something terrible were to happen to her. He remembered his isolation after Hank died, the agony of feeling as though he were the only person left in the world. He could not face that again. That scar had never healed until Marcella came into his life and closed his wound of loneliness with her love.

The walled city came into view. This village was different than the others he had seen. The battlements and huge gate were like a fortress, so the place reminded him of the medieval storybooks he had read as a child. The structure evoked thoughts of enemies held back time after time while trying to scale the great stone walls or break through the fortified gate. Great stone towers rose above the village and gave the skyline a spiked and ominous appearance.

Teresa parked in the lot outside the walls and Randy went over his plan with her one more time before they left the car and walked through the gated entrance to the town. Teresa had been there many times and knew exactly where to go. As they entered the gate, the narrow cobblestone street ahead was full of shops selling foods and souvenirs. Teresa led Randy through the shops and into a large piazza. The tallest structure in this small Renaissance town, the Torre Grossa, lay just ahead. The museum sat at the bottom of the giant stone tower, and they wandered around the back to the rear entrance. Nearby signs stated that the building was closed for renovations, so the place was empty.

Randy tried the door and it was unlocked as Nunzio had promised. He took the .45 from his waistband and pulled the slide back, chambering a round, but he left the safety on. Cocked and locked, as Hank would say, he took the .38 and tucked it in his waistband behind his back with the grip clearly exposed for quick removal. They entered the building and found the entrance to the staircase that led up to the bell tower. The tower itself was over two hundred feet tall so the climb would not be easy. He led the way with Teresa close behind.

Randy suspected that Nunzio chose this place for two reasons. First, he could see them coming and would know if they had brought the police. Second, with the tower closed to the public his prey would be alone so he could kill them without witnesses.

As they climbed flight after flight Randy kept Teresa close. When they neared the top he turned to her and kissed her cheek. "Just in case," he thought to himself. The last flight was a ladder that led through a small opening to the observation deck. Randy stopped and released the safeties from both weapons. He glanced back at Teresa once more and gave her a reassuring smile; she returned it weakly.

When he was halfway up the ladder his head was through the opening and he could see onto the deck, but only on one side of the bell which hung from the center. He would have to go around the bell to see the other side, where he was sure Nunzio was waiting for them.

The angry, insistent wind pulled at his Stetson and almost snatched it from his head so he took it off and handed it to Teresa. She tossed it to the bottom of the ladder. He took Teresa's hand and helped her up. She was breathing a little heavily from the climb, or maybe it was from fear. From this side they could see the entire city and far beyond. A wide, waist-high stone wall embedded with a rusted heavy steel cable encircled the deck.

Slowly Randy rounded the ancient bronze bell, and as he did two figures came into view. Against the back wall, facing him, were Marcella and Nunzio. His casted right arm held her waist, and with his left arm across her chest he held a long blade to her throat. A light trickle of blood ran down her neck from a small cut.

"*Bienvenuti,* Cowboy!" Nunzio said loudly with a big smile. "The view from here is truly magnificent is it not?"

"Randy?" Marcella pleaded.

"Don't worry, Marcella. Everything will be okay."

"Will it now?" Nunzio asked not really expecting an answer.

"I knew you were a coward, Nunzio, but this is a low point even for you. If you hurt her I'll kill you. You can be sure of that." Randy did his best to project strength but obviously Nunzio was calling his bluff. He laughed at Randy.

"You have done well fooling us all with your empty threats and machismo, Cowboy. You are a *frode*, a fraud. I now know you do not have it in you to kill. *I* on the other hand am more than willing."

Randy knew Nunzio would have no problem with killing if it suited his needs because he was a true sociopath.

"I see you have brought your big gun with you. Too bad you will not get a chance to use it."

Randy gripped the .45 so tightly the muscles in his forearm tensed visibly and his knuckles went white.

"This will make a bigger hole in your head then that pea shooter I took from you and threw away." Randy desperately hoped Nunzio would believe this lie.

"I am sorry to hear that. I was quite fond of that pistol and was hoping to have it returned to me." Nunzio's tone became serious now with no trace of his usual sarcasm.

"Now, you will place your gun on the floor and slide it over to me with your foot. Do it very slowly, Cowboy."

Randy hesitated. If his plan did not work he would be giving up his only means to protect himself and the women he loved.

"*Ora!* Now!" Nunzio yelled, and he held the sharp knife tightly to Marcella's neck so a new trail of blood began to run. She gasped at his tightened grip and the renewed pressure of the blade on her throat.

"Okay! Okay! Take it easy. I'm putting the gun down. Just don't hurt her. " Randy's voice sounded like a plea for mercy, but he knew he would receive none.

Nunzio smiled broadly now.

"Not so brave now, are you, Cowboy?" He knew he had won. "You thought you could come here with your stupid hat and boots and we would all cower like children watching westerns at the Saturday afternoon matinee."

Randy began to squat straight down very slowly with his gun extended as he was placing it on the floor. Teresa stood close, directly behind him. From his lowered position Randy looked up into Marcella's terrified eyes and said, "You will always be in my top ten Marcella." He furrowed his brow to be sure she realized what she must do now. She must remember. Their lives depended on it. Her eyes widened as she caught his meaning. Recognition registered on her face and he knew that she understood.

She raised her right elbow and drove it hard into Nunzio's ribs. The knife came away from her neck as he doubled over. She leaned away, straining to get free, but he still had her in his grip with his casted arm.

In that instant Teresa took the pistol from Randy's waistband at his back, pointed it at Nunzio as he was recovering, and, to his shock, she fired. Her shot went wide and she missed him completely, but Randy used the distraction to give him the precious seconds he needed. Standing in front of Teresa, he raised his father's .45 and shot Nunzio Salvatore through his left eye. A crimson mist of blood and brain matter rode the wind off the tower as the bullet exited his head.

The force of the large caliber weapon drove Nunzio's corpse beyond the wall and he disappeared over the edge. But his casted arm was still locked around Marcella's waist and when he went over his dead body's weight took her with him. She screamed as she began to fall. Randy saw this unfold in slow motion and dove toward the wall but missed her by inches. With one hand, Marcella grabbed the rusted steel cable that ran along the wall and caught herself before she could join Nunzio's body in its deadly freefall. Hanging on for dear life, she swung, screaming, two hundred feet from the ground.

Randy rushed to the wall and leaned over as far as he dared, seizing Marcella's hand just as she lost her grip on the cable. Now he had the full weight of her body drawing him too close to the edge and he could feel himself being pulled over.

"Teresa! Grab my legs!" he yelled as loud as he could, but his voice seemed weakened as it went out and over the wall, lost in the wind. He then felt her weight on his legs as Teresa grabbed them frantically. Her added weight stopped the deadly slide toward the rim of the wall and he shouted to Marcella, "Give me your other hand! Now!"

Randy reached as far as dared and Marcella swung wildly with her free arm for Randy's large outstretched hand. At last their hands connected and Randy squeezed as hard as he could even though he felt the bones of her fingers collapse under his vise-like grip. He would break them if he had to but he would not let her fall.

She winced at the pain but said only.

"Do not let me go, Cowboy!"

"Never!" Randy shouted with a straining voice.

There was fear in her eyes, yes, but also trust. She had faith Randy would not let her fall, so she did not panic.

As he struggled to pull her up, Randy looked past Marcella to the roof below. He could see Nunzio on his back in a growing pool of blood, his arms and legs splayed wide, perched on the shattered clay tile roof of the building some one hundred and fifty feet beneath her feet.

"Use your legs against the wall and push up if you can!"

As Randy strained to pull her up, Marcella helped herself by using some of the cracks in the stone for leverage. Slowly she reached the top of the wall until her weight was no longer pulling her downward. Randy reached for her shoulders, hauling her over the wall and onto the floor of the deck. All three were silent except for their heavy breathing. They lay on the floor of the bell tower, holding each other each silently thanking God for choosing not to take them this day. Randy had his arms tightly wrapped around the two people he loved most in this world. His family was safe now that was all that mattered to him.

As they rose to their feet Teresa said, "I'm sorry Randy, I missed him. Shooting a man is much harder than shooting a tree."

"That's all right, Mom. You were perfect. Killing should never be easy, but sometimes it just has to get done," he said still panting. Catching his breath, he found his spent .45 shell and tossed it from the opposite side of the observation deck, where it landed anonymously in a sea of tile roofs. "The police will be here soon and we must be prepared for what we will tell them," he said. "Let's get down there."

When they reached ground level Randy hurried to the car, hid the .45 in the trunk, and returned to the scene just before the *polizia* arrived.

Marcella explained to the police in Italian how Nunzio had kidnapped her at gunpoint and planned to kill them all. How Randy had fought with him and Nunzio had dropped his gun in the struggle. Teresa went on to explain that she picked up the gun and shot him with it while Randy pulled Marcella to safety. The first shot missed but the second did not. She handed the police Nunzio's unloaded pistol with two shots fired and the remaining bullets that Randy had removed from the weapon. This would explain all the fingerprints on the gun to the police. It was a plausible story as long as they stuck to it.

The police worked at removing Nunzio's broken body from the roof. Randy and the two women were escorted to the *posto di polizia*, the police station, for more questioning. They naturally focused on Randy in the investigation. As a foreigner involved in the death of an Italian citizen, he was heavily scrutinized. Teresa and Marcella stood by their story and Randy described the same events through an interpreter. After several hours of interrogation all were finally allowed to leave, but they took Randy's passport and told him not to try and leave the country until they had concluded their investigation. They would be in contact soon.

The *polizia* returned them to their car and left them there. Marcella turned to Randy and wrapped her arms around his neck.

"Too bad, Cowboy but I guess you cannot leave Italy without your passport," she said with a mischievous look.

"Damn. I was hoping to catch the next flight to Texas. Italy is just way too exciting for me," he said jokingly.

"Besides, if I ever have to save you from falling off a high tower again you are going to have to lay off the pasta."

This earned him another sharp poke in the ribs.

Chapter 36

The police visited the ranch several times for further questions, but it was becoming clear to them that the Conti women and Randy were telling the truth about the death of Nunzio Salvatore. After all, the man did have a record of violent offenses and had done time in prison on an attempted murder conviction.

The only witnesses they could find were those that heard the two shots fired from Nunzio's .38 and the two spent cartridges in the gun validated that story along with the fingerprint evidence. The motive for the kidnapping and attempts on their lives was still unclear to the detectives, and they did not like that lose end. However, it was evident who the criminal was and who the victims were in this case. They eventually returned Randy's passport and informed the group that the investigation was officially closed.

Teresa had spent much of the past week preparing for the meeting of the ranchers of Toscana. She and Enzo visited other families to ease their fears about the possible breeding plan. A few were adamant about maintaining the traditions of the past but most were open to the new possibilities of the program and of the financial benefits. By the time the day of the meeting arrived Teresa was convinced the plan would pass a vote.

Roberto Graso was uncharacteristically silent following the death of his strong-arm man. The police had asked him a few questions about his deceased employee but Graso played dumb very well. The police could establish no connection to him and the crimes of the dead man so they assumed he acted alone and that's exactly what Graso wanted them to think. So he made no more threats and kept to himself. He had lost his chance and he knew it. There was no sense in fighting a battle that was already lost and running the risk of implicating himself.

The day of the ranchers' meeting in Arezzo arrived. Teresa and Randy were up early as usual, having their morning coffee together.

"I called Tony last night and he told me you got an offer on the ranch in Calvert," Randy said while sipping his coffee.

"Yes, and it is a very good offer too, so I plan on accepting it." Teresa looked down at her cup as she spoke.

"You don't seem too happy about selling," Randy said. He could see the uncertainty in her face.

"It's just that selling Carl's dream does not feel right."

She looked up at Randy and he said, "Believe me. I know *exactly* what you're feeling."

Once again his and Teresa's life paths were strikingly similar. Randy was thinking about Hank's ranch and how it was at the center of his dreams as well. Strange how he now thought of it as his father's ranch and not his own any longer. It was obvious to him Teresa felt the same way.

"If it makes you feel any better I think you're doing the right thing. Carl would have wanted you to move on with your life and be happy."

"*Grazie mi figlio.* Teresa said, and this time she kissed the milk foam from his nose.

After Enzo and Teresa left for Arrezzo Randy went out to the barn and saddled one of the horses. He rode out onto the dirt service road until he came to the weedy rutted drive that led to the old ruined farmhouse. He tied off the horse and walked around to the courtyard that gave him the best view of the Val di Chiana, the place that had stolen his heart. He was more at peace now that at any other time since Hank's death. Even after all that had happened, his love of this ruined house and the surrounding lands had grown with each passing day.

Randy wandered through the dilapidated house, going from room to room. "Marcella loves this place," he thought. "It's her dream home." He stood in the large empty living room where they first made love. The dusty floor betrayed their secret, leaving visual proof of where they had laid together. The imprint of their bodies that remained in the dust took him back to that wonderful day.

Randy left the house and sat under the olive tree near the pond. He thought of his life in Montana and how lonely his time was there. He thought of his ranch in Calvert and how cut off he would feel there when he returned. He would be left with nothing but memories of the time he spent in Tuscany. The loneliness would be much worse now that he knew what it was to love someone and to be separated from her, maybe forever.

How abandoned and alone Hank must have felt when the woman he loved with all his heart left him with an infant to raise, a constant reminder of the short life they shared and the love he once held in his heart for her.

If Randy went back he would be destined to wear those same boots and be reminded with every step of what he had lost.

"Hold on to the ones you love Randy."

Hank's voice spoke to him once more.

"I know, Dad, but that means letting you go," he said aloud. As his eyes filled, a few tears fell on the grass and disappeared between the blades.

It was the middle of the night back in Texas but he needed to talk with Tony. He left the farmhouse and rode back to the villa to call his brother.

That evening Teresa returned from her meeting in Arrezzo. Randy heard her come in and went downstairs to hear the decision of the ranchers of the Val di Chiana. Teresa was pouring herself a glass of wine when he came into the kitchen.

"Care to join me Randy?" she said as she poured.

"As a matter of fact I would."

Randy smiled as she handed him a glass of Conti Famiglia Chianti. They raised their glasses.

"What are we toasting to?" Randy said as he held up his glass.

"To the fulfillment of Carl's dream to bring the Chianina to America!" she toasted.

Randy smiled as he touched her glass with his and said, "To Carl Swanson!"

Teresa and Randy sat at the breakfast table, sipping wine as she told him of the meeting. The ranchers had decided almost unanimously in favor of allowing the Chianina breeding program to move forward. Roberto Graso and a few others made one last effort to block the decision but he was overwhelmingly out voted. They would start small with only a few crossbreeds at first and then if successful would open up to other breeders. Soon, as Carl predicted, the Chianina would be available everywhere.

"Bistecca Fiorentina will be on the menu at all the best steakhouses in America," Randy joked, and they touched glasses once more.

Then he told Teresa about his conversation with Tony today.

"Tony told me that the Calvert ranch sold and the deal will close in a month," he said.

"Yes. Escrow closes quickly when the buyer pays cash."

"He also said that they asked about my place and are interested in buying it too."

"What will you do, Randy?"

"That depends a lot on you, Teresa."

"You are *famiglia*, Randy. You must know that by now, after everything we have been through together. I love you as if you were my own son. You will always have a place here with us."

Randy smiled and said, "I thought you would never ask." He rose and came around to Teresa and hugged her from behind and kissed her cheek. "I love you, too, Mom."

The next day he asked Marcella to go riding with him. They took the horses down the service road and on to the ruined farmhouse. Randy was quiet and Marcella respected his silence, so they spoke very little.

They left the horses and stood holding hands in the courtyard.

"I just wanted to come out here and see it like this, one more time with you," Randy said as he faced the old stone house.

"I am coming with you to Texas, Randy," Marcella announced firmly.

"No, you are not, Marcella. This is your home and this place is your dream. I will not let you give it up."

She let go of his hand took a step back and put her hands on her hips.

"I told you once before Randy that I do not take orders from you!" She was angry now. "I will not allow you to make decisions for me!"

Randy could not help himself and started laughing.

"What is so funny, Cowboy?" Marcella was fuming now. The more he laughed the angrier she got and the angrier she became the more he laughed. Finally she could control her temper no longer and began slapping and punching him. Randy picked her up, laid her across his shoulder and began to walk to the front door of the house.

"Put me down Randy!" she repeated every few steps. She was kicking her legs and slapping his back until finally they were inside and he set her down on the dusty tile floor. They stood now in the large living room. She was breathing heavily and her face was red and twisted with rage. Her raven black hair was wild as though she were caught in a terrible windstorm. Even like this she was beautiful to him. God, how he loved her.

"Marcella! Calm down! I came out here today to see this place like this one more time because it won't be like this for long."

"What do you mean, Randy? What are you talking about?" Now she was confused as well as angry.

He reached out and took her hands.

"I am selling my ranch in Texas and using the money to rebuild this house. I want to marry you Marcella and raise a family here with you. Your dream has become mine."

Her anger melted. Her face went from one extreme to the other. Rage was replaced with joy.

"Are you sure that is what you want, Randy?"

"More sure of it than I have ever been about anything in my life. Will you marry me Marcella?"

She jumped up on him, wrapped her legs around his back and hung from his neck.

"You have kept your promise to me, Randy, and I love you for it. Yes, Cowboy. I will marry you."

She kissed him now in this house as she had on that first day. This time there was nothing to hold her back.

Randy called Tony that night and asked him to handle the sale of his ranch.

"Mail me whatever I need to sign. Then you can bring the final papers yourself next month when the escrow closes Tony. I need my brother to be my best man."

"I would be honored, Randy."

September passed quickly in Toscana. Marcella was busy arranging the harvesting and crushing of the grapes and Randy was bringing the rest of the cattle down from the hills before the cold weather arrived.

The fall brought the colors of the turning season and the vines were afire with the red, yellow and gold leaves. The days were still warm but the nights and mornings brought a chilly reminder of winter's inevitable return.

Soon the olive harvest would begin and with it much hard work but also much celebration and gratitude for nature's gifts. Every town and village in Toscana would celebrate with festivals. It was also the perfect time for a wedding.

As the wedding day approached, Tony arrived, and Teresa and Randy were excited to see him, especially since the old Tony had come back from his dark swim in the pool of anger and despair. He looked forward to living again and this had lifted the sadness the family was forced to live with these past years.

Randy was in the barn when he heard the diesel roar of a large truck and trailer coming up the service road. The truck went just past the entrance to the driveway and began backing in. It backed up to the barnyard and stopped, the driver shut down the smoky motor and got out. As he did, a taxi appeared in the driveway. Randy recognized the smiling passenger in the back seat. His brother had finally come. He rushed the car and threw open the door. Randy reached in and bear hugged Tony as he laughed heartily. The taxi driver removed Tony's wheelchair and luggage from the trunk and Randy helped his brother into his chair just as Teresa came running from the house.

"Mi figlio!" she said as she wrapped her arms around him.

Tears and laughter mixed as the family reunited for the first time since those terrible last days when the tragedy of Carl's death had almost destroyed them all.

Marcella and Enzo walked up from his cottage down the road when they saw the large truck. Marcella welcomed Tony with kisses on his cheeks.

"No wonder you didn't come back, Randy!" Tony said as he looked at her. "How did an ugly cowboy like you land such a gorgeous woman?"

"It was his Texas charm!" Marcella laughed.

"Oh, right!" Tony returned with laughter. "He has all the charm of one your bulls I saw coming in!"

"What's the truck for, Tony? More luggage?" Randy smiled. He was curious about what Tony needed such a vehicle for.

"It's a wedding present, Brother." Tony said this as if he were a ringmaster about to introduce the next circus act.

"But first for your entertainment I must perform my greatest feat! And I do mean feet." Tony leaned over and removed the slippers he was wearing exposing his withered feet.

"Now watch closely ladies and gentlemen." Everyone was quiet and watched as Tony began to wiggle his toes, first on his right foot, then his left.

"Ta Da!" he sang loudly with a huge smile.

"*Grazie a Dio!* Thank God!" Teresa screamed, and she hugged her son with tears streaming from her eyes.

"Tony why did you not tell us this wonderful news?" she pleaded.

"I wanted to be sure it was for real before I told you." he said. "For the past few weeks I have been getting these strange tingling sensations in my legs so I went to see the doctor. He stuck me in the bottom of my foot with a needle and I almost jumped out of my chair!" Tony laughed out loud.

"Then a few days ago I could move my toes and feel hot and cold on my legs! The doctor said since my spinal cord was not severed in the accident the nerves are slowly restoring themselves and thinks with physical therapy and time I may even be able to walk again."

He beamed with happiness.

Teresa hugged him once more and Randy could not wait for her to get out of the way so wrapped his big arms around them both.

Randy looked at Tony with wet eyes and said.

"That's the best wedding present I could have ever hoped for, Brother!"

"That was only half the present! This is the other half!" He waved to the truck driver and the man opened the big doors of the truck. He pulled out two steel ramps that crashed to the ground on one end with the other attached to the cargo bed. The man climbed up the bed and into the dark cargo hold. Randy heard the sounds of heavy chains and the starting of a motor. He watched in disbelief as Hank's white and rusted Chevy pick-up rolled into view. The driver brought it down the ramps and into the barnyard and got out. Randy could not move. He stood there staring at the truck with his eyes wide and mouth open.

"It took a little to get her going but she purrs like a kitten now. Even has new tires." Tony said.

Randy slowly walked up to his father's pick-up truck and reached for the door handle. It stuck, so he had to give it a yank, as usual, to open it. There on the seat were his grandfather's Gibson guitar and Hank's black felt Stetson. The ash tray was still full. Tony had not had it cleaned out.

Randy brought his hands to his face and wept. He did not want to be seen like this, so faced only the open door of the truck away from everyone. He felt arms around him as he tried desperately to stop but it was useless. He gave into the emotion as Marcella was there holding him. Then Teresa joined them. Tony wheeled over, reached out to his brother and Randy took his arm.

In that moment Randy realized that he did not have to let go of Hank. He could hold his father in his heart forever and still have his new family at his side. He was overcome by joy and forgiveness. He had finally rid himself of the guilt he had carried for so long and allowed himself to love, and more importantly, to be loved by others. He would hold on to his family and never let go.

Hank had taught him this one final lesson.

That night they sat at the dining room table with a bottle of wine and signed all the necessary legal documents for the sale of the Swanson and Bartlett Ranches. Other papers needed to be reviewed as well. Tony had done most of the work but had some questions he needed to ask Teresa.

"Mom," he said to Teresa. "I found this letter from Malcolm Farley concerning the cattle he purchased from us a year after the accident." He read it out loud.

Dear Mrs. Swanson,

First let me say how sorry I was to hear of Carl's passing. I held him in high regard both as a rancher and a gentleman.

The cattle I purchased from you were in excellent condition and I am completely satisfied with the transaction.

However, I did want to ask you about one of the young bulls from your herd. He shows certain characteristics that I have never seen in an Angus bull and was wondering if you could tell me more about the stud you used to breed him. The bull is taller and more muscular than any I have ever seen and has some odd coloring and markings.

Please give me a call when you get a chance.

Thank you,
Malcolm Farley
Farley Ranch
Calvert, Texas

Tony put down the letter and looked at Teresa. Randy stared at her too and waited for her to respond.

Teresa grinned at them both. Her eyes showed both slyness and glee when she said, "I told you Chianina bulls reach puberty quickly. I guess we did not separate him from the herd soon enough."

Randy started laughing and Tony joined him. The thought of a young Chianina crossbreed bull mixed in with the Farley herd was just too ironic. Carl got his wish after all, just not the way he had planned.

Once again they raised their glasses to him.

Author's Note:

The ***record*** shows that the first American Chianina-Angus crossbreed was born on January 31, 1972 on a ranch near King City California.